---- ★ ----

She knew her time was running out. Her pulse was weak and thready without her Lanoxin. If Joe didn't kill her, her tired heart soon would. She wondered for the millionth time where Leroy was and if he was worried about her. She hoped Allison was all right. None of this was her fault. Allison had been a good, kind neighbor and now she might be in danger.

Malvina tried to ignore the pain as it grew into a crescendo, across her chest, down her left arm, up into her shoulder blade.

Her last conscious thought was to wonder how Joe would dispose of her body.

---- ★ ----

VALLEY OF DEATH

HELEN GOODMAN

W**O**RLDWIDE®

TORONTO • NEW YORK • LONDON
AMSTERDAM • PARIS • SYDNEY • HAMBURG
STOCKHOLM • ATHENS • TOKYO • MILAN
MADRID • WARSAW • BUDAPEST • AUCKLAND

Dedicated to the members of the
Anson County Writers' Club:
My friends, my mentors.

Recycling programs
for this product may
not exist in your area.

VALLEY OF DEATH

A Worldwide Mystery/September 2009

First published by Alabaster Books.

ISBN-13: 978-0-373-26686-9

Printed in U.S.A.

Acknowledgments

Many thanks to members of my critique groups:
Nancy, Betty, Dorothy, Diane, Dave
Dixie, Larry, Lynette, John, Emogene, Joanne, James.
Special thanks to Patty for proofreading these papers.

ONE

THE STONE HURTLED through the narrow window adjacent to the front door. Instead of the crashing noise the intruder had expected to hear, it was more of a tinkling sound as small pieces of glass slipped onto the tiled hall floor. Either way it didn't matter; no one else was close enough to hear. The school was separated from the rest of the town by a football field, a gymnasium, and two parking lots. The only neighbors lived across the street, their windows sealed tight against the cold January dawn.

No alarm sounded. The security system was as old as the school, and had been easily disconnected. A gloved hand squeezed through the broken glass enlarging the opening. Soon it was big enough to crawl through, and the intruder entered Madison Middle School.

A FEW BLOCKS AWAY, unaware that her classroom was being searched, Allison Aldridge stretched lazily on her sofa and sipped French Roast coffee. The aroma tickled her nose as the caffeine propped up her eyelids. It was a workday morning, but she'd arisen early and so had time to relax. Her bare toes caressed the orange cat sprawled at her feet. Although she was short *and* middle-aged, she had maintained her slim, athletic body through the years, so there was plenty of room on the couch for both her and the cat. Lancelot glanced up at her, gave a barely audible purr, and resumed grooming his left foreleg. His manner, though not haughty, conveyed the message that he had more important things to do than play with her toes. Allison sighed, reached for the local paper and her reading glasses.

The *Holliston Weekly Journal,* delivered on Tuesday afternoons, seldom contained any news which hadn't already made the gossip rounds in town, but Allison enjoyed reading the details and looking at the pictures. She'd been too busy correcting exam papers the night before to read much of it. Now she took the opportunity. She smiled at the wedding picture of a former student, nodded approval at the police crackdown on speeders, and noted the upcoming art show. Of course, she'd already jotted the art show in her Day-Planner since she always volunteered to help with the annual event.

She flipped to "State Notes" and read the headline aloud, *"Murder Rate Decreases in Urban Areas."* Glancing at the cat, she added her own comment, "About time the cities got some good news." But she was glad she lived in the small town of Holliston, the type of town Mark Twain would find familiar, *"town sleeping in a valley by a winding river."* Not Camelot, but close: peaceful, quiet, neighbors caring for neighbors, a place where a woman, like herself, was not afraid to live alone. Reading further, Allison frowned. "Wouldn't you know, Lancelot, this is an example of good news-bad news." The cat, interrupting his all-important grooming, raised one ear, cocked his head, and purred encouragement. "Listen to this, *'Conversely, murders have increased in rural areas and small towns.'*" Allison dropped the paper, picked up Lancelot, stroked him lightly. He was a dignified cat who disliked being snuggled or smooched. Allison understood this and usually respected his wishes, even though there were times when she felt the need of a good snuggle.

She acquired Lancelot last summer and transformed him from an outside cat who liked to sneak indoors into an inside cat who delighted in sneaking out. There's just no pleasing some critters, she mused, but she didn't hold it against him. He'd become a friend and confidant, someone to talk to other than herself. "Anyway," she informed him, "we don't have to worry. There hasn't been a murder in this part of North Carolina as long as I can remember."

Two staccato car honks interrupted their one-sided conversation. Allison carefully deposited Lancelot on the floor and headed for her bedroom. "Time for me to get moving," she said. With a neighbor like Leroy Hastings she didn't need a clock in the morning. The Hastings had lived next door to Allison for five years, and every weekday morning at exactly six-thirty, Leroy tooted goodbye to his wife, Malvina, as he drove off to work.

Allison's thoughts remained on Malvina through a quick shower and a poached egg breakfast. She stuffed her students' test papers in a tote bag bearing a Hilton Head Island logo. At the same time she pictured her homebound neighbor surrounded by a collection of travel magazines. Malvina was probably now staring out her front window watching the houses empty as their occupants hustled off to work or school. Soon the street would be deserted, leaving her to keep a lone vigil over the neighborhood.

Allison pitied Malvina, but also felt a touch of envy for her. Malvina had no children, little money, and a grave heart condition, but she did have Leroy, her husband of nearly forty years. Allison, on the other hand, had good health, an adequate income, two great kids in college. What Allison didn't have, was a man around the house. Her husband had abandoned his family, apparently without a backward glance, when the children were still toddlers. Malvina might have her lonely days, but Allison had the lonely nights.

ALLISON PARKED IN HER usual space across from the front drive of the long, low, redbrick school building. She collected her purse and her tote bag, pulled her coat collar up over her ears. Her short haircut was perfect for her job as the gym teacher, but did little to protect her head from the chilly breeze.

One of the other teachers was standing by her car, staring at the front entrance. Allison waved. "Good morning, Deb. The wind's a trifle brisk, wouldn't you say?"

Deb didn't answer, but pointed to the drive. "Wonder what's with the police car?"

"Oh, oh. Mr. Forster must have his tail in a knot again," Allison said. "What do you suppose it is this time?" The principal was well known to the Holliston police. He'd called them when Halloween pranksters had strewn toilet paper on the schoolyard trees, when overzealous football fans had burned the opposing team's mascot in effigy, and when someone had painted over the Ms in the school sign. Frankly, Allison thought, "adison iddle school" didn't sound horribly inappropriate.

Several other teachers soon arrived. Met at the front door by Alvin Forster, they were refused admission. The principal was a little man: short, spindly, who, in all like-lihood, had once been called "Peewee." Maybe he still was behind his back, but his reputation for enforcing every school rule and handing out stiff punishments instilled a certain amount of fear in both students and faculty. The teachers and other staff people were on a first name basis, but Mr. Forster was *Mister* Forster to everyone.

"I called 9-1-1," Allison heard him explain to the two uniformed officers, "as soon as I saw the broken win-dow. My secretary and I checked both our offices. Nothing seems to have been disturbed. I haven't had time to look elsewhere. But with the things happening in schools nowadays…." His voice trailed off.

"Just leave the looking to us," the older officer said.

His voice was brusque, but his eyes revealed uneasiness.

Allison felt her stomach crunch as she studied the somber faces surrounding her. A rising murmur of anxiety fluttered around the teachers.

"Everybody wait here until we get things checked out," the officer continued. "We need to get a detective and a crime scene crew out here. Can't be too careful these days with anything involving schools." He turned to his partner. "Go have a look around while I call in. Be careful."

"Yes sir." The young officer pulled on latex gloves, opened the door carefully and called back, "Reckon we'll need a bomb squad?"

A shock went through Allison's body. Surely they're overreacting, she thought. This has to be just a prank, or maybe some spiteful vandalism. Nothing more. Nothing to panic about. She kept telling herself this as they waited for the other police officers to arrive.

It didn't take long. Steve Pritchard, a young detective, introduced himself to everyone and took charge. Allison remembered Steve as a student. At that time he wanted to be a pilot, a professional wrestler, or a big game hunter. Allison didn't know what had led him into law enforcement, but it seemed to fit him perfectly. She'd followed part of his career from the local paper: his promotions, his move from uniform cop to detective, his work with the Civilian Police Academy. He still looked like an overgrown Boy Scout with his eager eyes, perfect posture, and determined chin.

He was polite and professional as he issued orders to his former principal. "We'll secure this area. You can let the staff in at another door. After we've gone over everything, please have the teachers check each of their classrooms for anything out of place." He turned to the teachers. "If you find anything wrong, let me know. Try not to touch or disturb anything." Allison and the others nodded.

As she started to leave, Allison turned to the detective. "It's good to see you again. But I'd like to know one thing."

"And that would be?"

"Do I address you as 'Detective Pritchard' or can I still call you 'Steve'?"

The detective laughed. "Steve is fine if you promise not to give me any more homework."

Since the students would be arriving soon, Mr. Forster suggested a plan for them. Someone would be assigned to meet the cars and buses and direct the students to the gym. It was too cold to have them wait outside. Steve agreed, but sent an officer to check out the gymnasium first to be sure it hadn't been entered by the intruder. Allison didn't know the other young man who was trailing Steve. He'd been introduced as Officer Gil Watts. He didn't look much older than her son, Dave, who was a sophomore at NC State. Both Dave and Gil retained traces of acne, a scattering of freckles, and a demeanor of assumed confidence. Right now he looked like Dave used to after he'd had a fight with the alarm clock: eyes at half-mast, hair hurriedly combed, shirt barely tucked in. Allison was glad this was only a break-in. She certainly wouldn't want Steve and this kid to be investigating anything like a murder.

She smiled as her thoughts swung to Fred Sawyer, the detective she'd met last summer during a murder investigation on her vacation. Now *there* was a mature, seasoned law officer. Working together they'd solved the case, had kept in touch, and were now very good friends. Perhaps, Allison thought, they might be more than just good friends. Things seemed to be moving in that direction. But for right now, she had to put Fred out of her mind and concentrate on the task at hand.

When she reached her classroom, Allison studied her domain. It took her a couple of minutes to realize something was out of order. The plaque on her desk reading, *"My peace I give to you,"* was turned toward the classroom. She was always careful to keep the plaque where she could see it, but facing away from the students. Sometimes she felt the need to be reminded of God's promise of peace, but didn't want to be accused of foisting her religious convictions on her students. It was tricky sometimes, in the present political climate, to adhere to certain principles without offending those who might disagree.

She now resisted the urge to turn the plaque around. Without touching anything, Allison scrutinized the rest of the room. She noticed that some papers on a shelf had also been disturbed. Instead of the neat stacks she maintained, they were jumbled and disarranged. She puzzled over what it all meant, and went to find Steve. What had the intruder been looking for—and why?

TWO

ALLISON WATCHED AS her desk and files were dusted for fingerprints. Steve admitted they had little hope of finding any that didn't belong there. "It's evident the intruder wore gloves," he told Allison. "There were no prints on the window where he entered."

"And our friend didn't mess up any of the other rooms?" Allison asked.

"Not that we can tell at this point. So-o, Mrs. Aldridge, we must assume that you had something he wanted." Steve winked at his former teacher and gave her a silly grin. "Got some kind of contraband hidden here?"

Allison smiled back. "Not since I confiscated your Jungle Girl comic books."

"Ouch, you do have a long memory." Steve brushed back his thatch of dark hair. "But you must have had something in here worth stealing."

"I can't imagine what."

"There has to be something. Would you go through your desk, your files, everything? Write down whatever's missing."

"Of course, Steve, but I tell you there's nothing here

that a student would be interested in. I took yesterday's test papers home to grade, but even if they'd been here, they're not important enough to steal. One test won't make or break a student."

"What makes you think it's one of your students?"

"Who else could it be? Only a student would know which room was mine if, as you say, I had something he wanted. There are no name plates on the doors."

Steve raised his eyebrows. "Mrs. Aldridge, how long have you taught health and PE here?"

"Fifteen years."

"How long have you had the same classroom?"

"Fifteen years."

"Exactly. I haven't been in your room in nearly twelve years, but I certainly haven't forgotten where it is. The intruder could be a *former* student, a parent, or even a former teacher. Or a friend of any of the above who gave him the necessary information. It's going to be impossible to find the culprit until we learn what he was after. Or she," Steve added. "I'm not ruling out a female. It's just easier to use the generic pronoun."

Allison laughed softly. "As I remember, you never did have a problem with giving girls equal opportunity. You flashed your beautiful smile at every one of them."

Steve let out a low chuckle and blushed slightly. "Yeah, I guess so. But now to get back to your assignment, Mrs. Aldridge. Mr. Forster is going to assign someone to keep your students busy until you finish your inventory. And I remember you telling us when we faced a particularly tough job, that the hardest part is getting started. So may I suggest you get started?"

Allison nodded. "I'm glad you remembered at least one thing I told you." She reached into her purse, got out her reading glasses, and got started.

About an hour later Steve and Mr. Forster came back to her classroom. Allison was ready with her report. "Nothing," she said. "There's absolutely nothing missing. Someone went through the desk drawers, the file cabinet, and the book shelves. I could tell because things were out of alignment. But I'm sure he didn't take anything."

"Strange," Mr. Forster said.

"The strangest part is that he seemed to have been most interested in the shelf where I keep old magazines and art supplies. I could tell that each item on that shelf had been removed and then replaced, but they weren't replaced in the order I had them."

Steve bent down and examined the shelf, picked up a gardening magazine, some poster paper, pictures of skeletons and of sports figures. "You're still having your students make posters for health class?"

"Sure. They love doing it. At least they seem to. Didn't you enjoy it?"

"Of course, it was very enlightening," Steve said. "You know it might even help me today. I could take a big piece of poster board, tape all my clues on it, and hang it in my office. It would be a real source of inspiration."

Allison shook her head at the detective. "I see you haven't lost your flair for sarcasm."

Mr. Forster was in no moods for jokes. "This is no laughing matter. The sanctity of our school has been violated. What do we do now?"

Allison had never thought of the school as sanctified, or its halls as hallowed. In the past she'd made jokes about their sports teams being called "The Little Demons." But she had to agree with the principal. This violation of her classroom was not a laughing matter.

Her voice trembled slightly as she echoed Mr. Forster's question. "What *do* we do now? What if he comes back?"

"The first thing the school needs to do is install a proper security system. It's something that should have been done years ago."

Mr. Forster nodded in agreement. "I'll get right on it. We'll get a security system with enough bells and whistles to scare off any burglar. Next time we'll be ready for him."

Allison shuddered as a new thought skittered into her brain. "What if the next time isn't here?"

The principal scowled at her. "What do you mean?"

"My room was the target. Steve said I must have something the burglar wanted. If that's so, then he might decide that since he didn't find it here, it might be at my house." She turned to Steve. "Tell me I'm crazy, that I don't have a thing to worry about."

"Wish I could," Steve said, "but you may be right. His next attempt might be your house. On the other hand, this case may be as simple as one student daring another. You know kids do that sometimes. But we can't take any chances, so I guess our next step is to check out your home security: the locks, the windows, the yard lights." Steve gave Allison that mischievous grin she remembered from another era. "I can't have anything happening to my favorite former teacher."

Mr. Forster took off his glasses and swiped his hands across his eyes. "What if the burglar is at Mrs. Aldridge's house this very moment?"

"I doubt that," Steve said. "Not in broad daylight."

"I agree," Allison said, "but what about when it's not broad daylight? I may not be able to sleep a wink tonight. You'd better check for goblins under my bed while you're at it."

"Will do. That is, if Mr. Forster will excuse you from school for a bit."

"Of course," the principal said. "Go. Do what you have to do. Right now I have to make a phone call. I was planning on going to St. Augustine this weekend, but in light of what's happening I think I should stay in town, so I'll cancel my reservations."

"You must really like Florida," Allison said. "You just spent the Christmas holidays in Miami."

Mr. Forster raised his pencil-thin eyebrows and gave her a look which she interpreted as, *"How dare you comment on my personal activities."*

She gave an apologetic shrug. "Of course it's none of my business."

"Precisely."

Steve stood up. "I'm afraid it may take a couple of hours. Can you spare her for that long?"

Mr. Forster fluttered both hands at them as if shooing away some pesky flies. "Take the rest of the day off if you wish, Mrs. Aldridge." The words were right, but the tone was wrong. Allison caught the underlying disapproval.

"That won't be necessary. I'll be back as soon as we've secured my premises." Allison mentally patted herself on the back for sounding so official and looked smugly at Steve. He nodded his approval.

"Besides," Allison went on, "the girls are playing basketball after school tonight. As their coach I can't miss the game." She shuddered as she suddenly realized what that meant. It would be late when she got home tonight. Even though Steve meant to assure her safety, she was still going to be entering an empty house—after dark—alone. She'd been doing it for years without trepidation, but now the thought of someone possibly lurking in the shadows gave rise to the cold creeps.

THREE

STEVE TOOK HIS TIME examining Allison's little brick bungalow. The windows were all locked and the tall azaleas that hugged the house made access to them quite difficult. A street light in front and a yard light in back were assets. He recommended she also keep the side porch light on. It would illuminate the carport and the kitchen door where she usually entered.

"I'd like to call a buddy of mine at Grant's Locksmith," he said. "You need dead bolts and chains on both the front and side doors, a bar across the back patio door, and your windows need to be secured better."

Allison appreciated his concern. She felt her anxiety slowly slipping away to be replaced with a sense of embarrassment. "I'm sorry I acted like such a scaredy-cat. It was silly of me since there's nothing valuable or sinister hidden in this house."

"That you're aware of, that is."

They were sitting at the kitchen table and Allison felt the need for coffee. Coffee's hot breath calmed her nerves, energized her, and enabled her to face whatever came next. "Would you care for some warmed-up coffee?" she asked. "It's left over from breakfast. I always make too much, but I have to have perked coffee in the morning and I can't perk just two cups. The directions say you can, but I've tried, and it just doesn't taste right." Allison realized she'd started jabbering, which she tended to do when she was nervous. Without waiting for an answer, she filled two mugs and placed them into the microwave.

"You're right, of course, about the locks," she said. "I want to take every precaution even though it's probably unnecessary. Call the locksmith. Have him put in every security device he can think of, short of a siren. I'm not sure I want an alarm system. It seems like a bit of overkill."

"Fine. If you can give me a spare key, I'll let him in so you can get back to school." The microwave beeped. "After we've had our coffee."

They sat in silence, hunched over steaming mugs, each lost in private thoughts. The cheery, lemon-yellow kitchen stood in sharp contrast to the solemn mood of its occupants. Steve raised his spoon after stirring in a dollop of non-dairy creamer. "Another thing we need to do is put a bolt on the door leading to the basement. That way if anyone did manage to get in down there, he wouldn't be able to get through to the rest of the house."

Allison could only nod as she felt her throat closing in terror. Her mind was racing back to last summer, to another basement, where she'd been trapped on the wrong side of such a bolt. She could again feel the heat and smell the smoke of the fire that had been intended to kill her. Steve, of course, had no knowledge of that close encounter, but he studied her with worried eyes. "I'm sorry. I don't mean to upset you. There's probably very little chance of the school intruder coming here. But it's my job, you know. We detectives tend to think of worst possible scenarios."

"I know," Allison said. "It's okay. I appreciate your help. I'll be getting back to school now. You'll check in with me when you finish here?"

"Sure. I'll see you later. Thanks for the coffee."

THAT EVENING, while Allison's girls were screaming over a missed basket, a different skirmish was going on in another part of town. Two men glowered at each other. "I tell you it wasn't there. I went over her desk, shelves, files." The young man spread his hands out to emphasize his words. "Zero. Zilch."

The older man grunted.

"That means it's at her house," the young man went on. "It's going to be tricky breaking in there. But it has to be done."

"Maybe not."

"You got another plan? Maybe I could just knock on the door, say I'm hungry, and she'll invite me in. Then when teacher's fixing me milk and cookies, I'll search the house." Sarcasm lingered on his taut lips. His black eyes challenged his older companion. "Dream on, you old geezer."

The older man studied his gnarled knuckles. "I'll handle it," he said.

"How?"

"Never mind how."

"Well, it was your stupidity that got us into this mess in the first place, so you'd better handle it and handle it good. And whatever you do, it's got to be soon."

"Couple of days."

"Fine. But if it doesn't work, then the ball is back in my court and I'll do anything I have to. Understand?"

"Understood."

THE DEFEAT OF the Lady Demons seemed an appropriate ending to a bizarre day. Allison wasn't even surprised when one of her girls sprained an ankle and another reported a severe headache. It seemed par for the course. Allison just wished the ball game over, and the day at an end.

When she left the gym, she was surprised to see Gil Watts waiting for her at the door. The young officer had changed from his uniform into black jeans and a black sweatshirt. She studied him warily as he approached her car. He must have seen the question in her eyes. "Thought I'd follow you home," he said. "It happens that my apartment is only a few blocks from your house."

"What an unexpected pleasure," Allison said. "It isn't often I get an escort home. Of course, it's not necessary. But it's nice." Allison gave him a motherly smile. "Nice car, too," she said, as they approached a shiny poppy-red Eldorado. "Policemen must make more money than teachers around here."

"Not likely," Gil said. He rubbed his hand tenderly over the hood. "Present from my pappy—for being a good boy."

Allison studied the young man in front of her. He had hair the color of dead leaves that matched his brown eyes, and his light eyebrows were barely discernable in a forehead too wide for the rest of his face. She imagined that being a good boy didn't come particularly easy for him. "You're not from Holliston, are you?"

"No ma'am. From Charlotte, but I wanted to get away from the city for a while. Thought I'd see what small town life was like."

"And what do you think of it?"

"Actually, it's not so different. There are some good people, some not-so-good people, and some downright bad people everywhere."

His answer surprised her. She hesitated as she unlocked her car. "You really think we have downright bad people here in Holliston, Officer Watts?"

"Afraid so, ma'am. And please call me Gil. You remind me of an old, I mean, former teacher of mine."

Allison laughed. "All right, Gil. And are you following me home because of the bad people, or because I'm like your old teacher?"

Gil grinned. "Both I guess. And since I'm one of the good guys, I figured you might not mind the company."

When Allison pulled into her carport, Gil was right behind her and climbed out of his car as she fiddled with the house key. She glanced at him over her right shoulder. "This is very nice of you, but you really don't need to come in."

"Oh, but I insist. I'm sure Steve would want me to check out your new locks." Allison shrugged and went in, with Gil at her heels. He rattled the front door lock, jiggled the bar across the patio door, slid the bolt on the basement door and peered into the darkness. "What's downstairs?"

"The furnace, Ping-Pong table, extra school supplies." She hung her coat in the hall closet. "Why?"

"I was just wondering where a burglar might look." His gaze combed the den, lingered briefly in the kitchen. He seemed satisfied and headed for the door. "Everything looks secure. By the way, who do you play Ping-Pong with?"

Allison laughed. "You certainly do ask some off-the-wall questions. Are you trying to play Columbo?"

"I'm sorry. I'm pretty new at this detecting game. Maybe I'm being too eager. Just want to be a good cop." Gil put both hands on the back of his neck and stretched. "Guess I'd better go."

Allison walked him to the door. "The answer to your question is: I don't play Ping-Pong, but my kids do."

Gil stopped with his hand on the doorknob. "Kids? You have kids here?"

"Not anymore, unfortunately. They're both in college, NC State. I won't see them again until Spring Break." She paused. "It seems like such a long time between their visits."

Gil's head bobbed up and down. "I know how that is. I don't get back to visit my mother very often either."

Allison patted his hand. "We mothers are a strange lot. We can't wait until our kids grow up and leave the nest, but as soon as they do, we want them home again." She backed away as Gil opened the door. "Good night, Gil. You'd better get some rest. You look tired."

"That's okay. I can sleep in tomorrow. It's my day off."

"Lucky you. Bye now. Thanks for caring."

It was only after Gil left that Lancelot greeted her with a warm ankle massage and a gentle purr. The cat didn't take to strangers, especially men. Allison locked and chained the door and gave a sigh of relief. She was in her safe little house now with nothing to worry about. She pushed the day's happenings to a hidden corner of her mind, pulled a chicken fricassee dinner from the freezer, and kicked off her shoes.

It was then she noticed the red light blinking on her answering machine and hoped it would be either Fred or one of her kids. No such luck. Allison winced as she heard her neighbor's voice. Malvina never gave her name, she didn't have to. No one else had such a perpetual whine. "Allison, call me as soon as you get home." A long pause was followed by, "It's important."

Allison sometimes wished she could ignore people's requests. Bone tired, with nerves on edge all day, she had no desire to listen to Malvina's complaints. She liked her neighbor, but she had learned long ago what

Malvina considered important. It could be anything from Mr. Wyman's dog digging up her iris bulbs to Channel 8 preempting her soap opera. She felt ashamed of herself and dialed the Hastings' number.

Leroy answered on the first ring. Allison asked for Malvina and was puzzled when Leroy answered, "Already in bed."

"Oh? She left a message for me to call. Could you check? Maybe she's not asleep yet." Allison knew that Malvina would often go to bed early and then read herself to sleep.

"She's asleep. Felt poorly." Leroy wasn't one to waste words. Even though she knew he was devoted to Malvina, Allison couldn't imagine them having in-depth conversations.

"I'm sorry she isn't feeling well. She said it was important she talk to me. Do you know what she wanted?"

"Nope. Check with her tomorrow."

"Yes. I'll do that. Thank you." Allison hung up the phone with a feeling of being reprieved. At least she didn't have to deal with her neighbor's problem tonight, whatever it might be.

She recalled their last meeting two days earlier. Malvina had called and left a message that she had something to give her. Allison had gone over after school, taking some chocolate chip cookies the band members were selling, and they spent nearly two hours talking over decaf. It was only when she was leaving that Malvina remembered the purpose of the visit. She heaved herself off the sofa, shuffled over to the corner desk and handed Allison a calendar of the previous year. "You said you could use these pictures for your health class."

"You remembered. How sweet of you." Allison had been delighted to get the calendar. Each month pictured a different healthful activity: walking a nature trail, bicycling, a backyard softball game. "These will be perfect for my students to use on their posters. Thanks ever so much."

Malvina smiled broadly showing teeth yellowed from years of smoking. Her cigarettes had been replaced with Juicy Fruit, which she smacked as she answered, "It's the least I can do. You're always doing favors for me."

Allison had meant to take the calendar to school the next day, but had forgotten. It now lay on the coffee table under the *Holliston Journal*. She picked the calendar up and gazed at a beach scene. She smiled at the children with sand buckets, the sun worshipers, the swimmers braving high surf. It wasn't difficult to erase a dozen years and see herself and her children on that same beach. On the calendar part, on the back of each picture, were the usual monthly appointments for Malvina, reminders of events, and some other scribbles. Allison tossed it back on the table, stifled a yawn and headed for bed.

FOUR

THE NEXT DAY WAS back to routine. The break-in, although not forgotten, wasn't the topic of every conversation. Mr. Forster told Allison at lunchtime that Steve had called, saying the police would stay on the case, but he didn't hold much hope for solving it. Allison sighed in resignation. "Oh well," she said. "No harm done. Maybe it was just a prank."

That afternoon there were no games, no meetings, no parent conferences to detain Allison after school. She was thankful for that because the weather was turning flat-footed nasty. She didn't need a weatherman to tell her the cold rain mixed with plummeting temperatures would soon result in icy streets. North Carolina winters are so capricious, she thought. Last year they had only two light snowfalls that disappeared by the next morning. This year, however, Old Man Winter seemed intent on testing their fortitude. "Okay by me," she muttered to the rain. "Just let me get home to my warm house and hot coffee."

Allison pulled into the carport, hurried into the house, and turned up the thermostat. She headed for the bedroom, peeled off her dress slacks and blouse and pulled on her oldest and warmest sweat suit. It had once been dark blue, but repeated washings had bleached it to a soft azure. She studied her reflection in the bathroom mirror as she brushed her low-maintenance, no color touch-up hair. It seemed as if a dozen more gray hairs had appeared overnight. If only my hair aged as nicely as this outfit, she thought, instead of looking like a dust mop left out in the rain. Allison recalled the conversation with her beautician the last time she had her hair cut.

"How about a little rinse?" June Ellen had asked. "Just enough to cover up those sneaky gray strands."

Allison shook her head. "I think salt-and-pepper hair looks distinguished."

"On men, it's distinguished. On women, it's aging."

Allison stared at the mirror. She rubbed her firm chin, smoothed out two tiny wrinkles between her eyebrows. Her face was still good, she thought, but maybe June Ellen was right. She was only forty-seven. She didn't want a few gray hairs to make her look like an AARP candidate. She looked over at Lancelot who was trying to make friends with the waste basket and said with exasperation, "But I have worse things than my hair to worry about now."

In spite of her best efforts, she wasn't able to blot out the picture of her ransacked classroom or ignore the fear that her home might be the next target. She rechecked the locks, zapped a cup of coffee, and tried to get her mind on something else. She dialed her neigh-

bor. After four rings, she heard Leroy's voice on the answering machine, "Hastings. Leave a message."

Allison knew it wasn't unusual for Malvina to take
a nap in the afternoon and ignore the phone. "Malvina,
this is Allison returning your call from yesterday. I'll
be home all evening. Call me when you get up if you
still want to talk." She hoped that whatever was so important to her neighbor yesterday no longer mattered.

The rain evolved into sleet. Allison settled down on
the sofa and propped pillows so she had a good view
of her backyard being slowly turned into an ice arena.
She pulled up her granny-square afghan, grateful she
didn't have to go out. Reaching for paper and pencil she
kept on the coffee table, she started scribbling lines of
poetry, which were bouncing around in her head. It
was a frequent happening. She had a reverence for
nature and for words, and often felt compelled to com-
bine the two.

Winter's jewelry:
Glistening, luminescent,
Fragile. Icicles.

She nodded in satisfaction. Haiku was one of her
favorite forms of poetry. One could say so much in just
a few syllables. She dropped the pad, and searched for
some reading material. She debated between a book
recommended by Mr. Forster, *Success in the Classroom,* or finishing *The Penthouse Murders.* It wasn't

much of a debate. Allison picked up the mystery book and turned to the page where she'd stopped reading a few days earlier, where the telephone was ringing in the empty penthouse. She suspected it was the murderer checking whether or not anybody was there before he returned to the scene of the crime. She settled back, reading with relish.

A couple of hours later she jumped as her own telephone shrilled. It was Leroy. Without preliminaries he announced, "Malvina's at sister's. Be gone a few days."

"In this weather?" Allison was perplexed. Malvina seldom went out even in good weather. She'd sold her car last year when the doctor advised her to give up driving. Leroy did their grocery shopping and errands. Malvina's sister, Faye, who lived in the next county, would take her out for lunch sometimes or come get her to stay a few days, but Allison couldn't imagine them out on a day like this.

Leroy gave her the explanation. "They had this planned. Left this morning. She'll call you when she gets back."

There seemed nothing else to say. "Sure. Well— thanks."

It was dark by now. She closed the blinds and turned on the TV. Her book would have to wait until after the weather report. Local weathermen loved days like this. It gave them a chance to talk about high pressure areas, wind chills, falling barometers, and possible school closings. It was the latter that interested Allison.

However, Mr. Meteorologist sadly predicted the freezing rain would end by midnight and temperatures would start rising. Allison could sense the disappointment of students throughout the district. The best they could hope for was an hour delay in school opening.

The newscaster rattled on about trouble in the Middle East, poor airport security, and scandals in Washington. So what else was new? Tuning out the world news, her mind turned to her neighborhood's news. Something wasn't right. Malvina hadn't told Allison anything about a visit to her sister. On Monday they'd talked about spring flowers, about upcoming TV specials, about the school Spring Break, even about the summer cruise Leroy had promised her for their anniversary. But nowhere in that potpourri of exchanges did Malvina mention Faye or an intended visit. And, Allison reminded herself, Leroy had told her the night before to "check with her tomorrow." If Malvina had planned a trip for the next day, wouldn't he have known about it?

Allison ate a roast beef sandwich, tossed the paper plate into the trash can, and chided herself for being silly. "Malvina doesn't have to tell me all her plans," she reported to Lancelot. The cat was too busy with his own kitty roast to answer. "Maybe Faye heard the bad weather was coming and didn't want Malvina to be alone. Yes, that makes sense." Allison felt better now that she'd come up with a logical explanation. She went back to her murder mystery and didn't think about Malvina again until the following afternoon.

FRIDAYS WERE ALWAYS long days. The students looked
forward to their extended curfews that night and their
Saturday sleep-ins, while teachers longed for weekends
of peace and quiet. The weather had cleared as predicted
during the day, but dark clouds scudded in from the west
as Allison started home. Street lights popped on unexpectedly and a blast of Arctic air announced another
winter storm on the way. Allison stopped at the supermarket. If she had to hibernate this weekend, she intended to do it on a full stomach. Of course, all the rest
of Holliston's inhabitants had the same idea. The store
was packed. The bread shelves were nearly empty, the
few gallons of milk left looked lonely, and batteries were
being snatched up faster than a blue-light special at
K-mart. Allison topped off her cart with the essentials:
Folger's, Snickers, and a Dell Crossword Puzzle book.

She didn't really mind being shut in for a while, but
she did hope the weather wouldn't force the cancella-
tion of the community art show Saturday evening. The
show meant a lot to local artists and was a major event
for the Art Council. As a member of the council, and
an art lover, Allison looked forward to it every year.

She arrived home, decided she needed nourishment
before fixing dinner, and was on her second brownie
when the phone rang. "Mrs. Aldridge?"

"Yes."

"Faye Latham here. Sorry to bother you."

"No bother. What can I do for you? Is Malvina well?"

There was a pause on the other end of the line, and

what Allison thought was a caught breath followed by Faye's soft voice. "But that's what I was going to ask you."

Now it was Allison's turn to catch her breath. "You mean she's not at your house?"

"No. I've been trying to call her all day, but keep getting the answering machine. I'm beginning to get worried—what with the weather getting worse and Leroy working late like he does on Fridays." Allison could hear the concern in Faye's voice. "Would you mind running over to check on her? I've left several messages for her to call me back. It's just not like her, you know."

Allison tried to keep the fear out of her own voice. "Malvina's not home, Faye. Leroy said she'd gone to visit you."

"Where did he get an idea like that? I haven't seen her in more than two weeks. The last time we talked I mentioned I might be over this weekend, but with the storm coming, I was going to tell her I couldn't make it." The ensuing silence left Allison's mind grasping for something to say. But Faye said it for her. "I'm afraid something may have happened to Malvina."

FIVE

ALLISON'S LIFETIME HABIT of trying to reassure people kicked in. "Now, I'm sure nothing has happened. I may have misunderstood Leroy. I'll go right over and check on her. Malvina gave me a key to the back door a long time ago. Now where did I put it? I've never had to use it, but I'll find it in case I need it. That is, in case Malvina can't get to the door." She took a deep breath. "Now don't worry. I'll call you back in a few minutes. Let me have your phone number."

Allison knew she hadn't misunderstood Leroy and she had a gut feeling Malvina was now or had been in terrible trouble. She found the key, pulled on her parka and started out. But fear clutched her stomach and her neighbor's key shook in her hand. Two thoughts raced through her mind. What if I don't find her? And then, what if I do find her and she's…. Allison couldn't even finish the last thought.

She turned and headed back to the phone. She wanted to call the police department directly in hopes that Steve would still be in his office. A few years ago she might have done that, but now Holliston had 9-1-1, and citizens were urged to follow protocol for any emergency. She wasn't sure this would qualify as an emergency, but she dialed the number and then felt a little foolish explaining she wanted a police escort just to check on a neighbor. The person taking the call, however, was kind and promised to send someone in a few minutes.

Allison waited nervously. It was Gil who drove up. She went over her story as they made their way to the Hastings' back door. His only comment was, "Life in Holliston is beginning to heat up a little."

Allison handed Gil the key and stepped back. He knocked and called and then unlocked the door. Allison switched on the light as she followed Gil in. It was still daylight outside, but the room was dark and gloomy. "Malvina," she called hesitantly as she scanned the kitchen. Everything looked normal except for a few dirty dishes in the sink. The den seemed undisturbed so they headed for the bedroom. It was as empty as the rest of the house.

"Nothing here," Gil said.

"Oh, but there is," Allison said as she stared at the unmade bed. "Malvina would never leave the house without making up the bed. And she wouldn't leave dirty dishes in the sink. She was almost compulsive about keeping her house neat and clean. Leroy was right about her not being here last night. He must have left the dirty dishes as well as the unmade bed."

"Or she was here and wasn't able to make up the bed or do the dishes." Gil scratched at a tiny scab on his left cheek and Allison resisted her motherly urge to warn him against picking his face. Gil scratched again and his voice lowered to an ominous level, "Or she's still here somewhere. That means we search everywhere—under, over and behind everything. I'm going to call for some help."

"And we've got to call Leroy," Allison said. "He'll be frantic when he learns something has happened to Malvina."

"Or," Gil said, "he may already know."

Allison regarded Gil's set jaw and hard eyes and revised her opinion of him. He's not an innocent youngster, she thought. He's seen his share of trouble, and he has known people at their worst.

"Where does he work?" Gil asked.

"He does maintenance work at the Valley Textile Mill. Want me to make the call?"

"Yeah. Tell him to get his tail home. Then call the sister back. Don't alarm her, but see if you can get any more information out of her. You know, husband trouble, money troubles, the whole gamut. She might be more likely to confide in you than the police."

Steve and two other officers arrived shortly. They were introduced as Martha Sullivan and Tim McCall. Allison noted they were probably in their early thirties, wore their uniforms proudly and answered Steve with quick "Yes Sirs," even though he was younger than they were.

Steve seemed uneasy. He turned to Gil. "Tell me

again why we're here. No one has reported a missing person. We have no search warrant or reason to obtain one. And you've been nosing around a private home without permission." Steve's voice became strident. "Just what do you think you're doing?"

Gil's face turned scarlet. "But Sir, Mrs. Aldridge called 9-1-1 and said her neighbor was missing and she is. That is, she's not here. At least there's no sign of her. That's why I called for a detective. Technically Mrs. Hastings has been missing for over twenty-four hours." Gil wiped his hand over his mouth and swallowed hard. "Well, that's what Mrs. Aldridge said, anyway."

Steve shook his head, Officer McCall fidgeted with his holster, and Officer Sullivan had a smirk on her face as if she were enjoying Gil's discomfort. Allison came to Gil's defense. "Gil's absolutely right. We do have a missing person. Her sister reported it to me and I reported it to the police department. There's nothing wrong with that. Now are you going to start looking for her?"

Steve gave Allison an apologetic smile. "Not until Mr. Hastings arrives and we hear his story. I appreciate your concern for a neighbor, but I just hope you haven't gotten all of us in deep doo-doo." He immediately blushed when he realized what he'd said. "I mean, Mr. Hastings could be upset with us for being here."

"I guess we'll soon find out," Allison said. "Here he comes now."

Leroy skidded into the driveway and slammed into the house. "What's going on here?" he demanded.

"That's what we'd like to know, Sir," Steve answered quietly. "We have a report that your wife is missing."

"Missing?" Leroy turned to face Allison, hands on his hips and fury in his face. "I told you she'd gone to her sister's. What kind of trouble you trying to cause?" Leroy was a scarecrow of a man: tall, gaunt, stringy gray hair protruding out from under a beige hunting cap, and wearing grimy coveralls which looked three sizes too big. The top of the coveralls were unsnapped in front revealing a blue-plaid flannel shirt. It looked like he had started to remove his outer garment and then changed his mind. Allison knew he'd never come in the house in those greasy coveralls if his wife were at home. She'd told Allison once that Leroy always removed his greasy clothes at work and brought them home in a plastic bag for her to wash. But Malvina wasn't here now to object as Leroy leaned his soiled sleeves on the kitchen counter and glared at his neighbor.

Steve stepped between Leroy and Allison. "Have a seat, Mr. Hastings. We need to talk."

Leroy yanked a chair out from the kitchen table and flopped. "Talk."

Allison wanted to say something to comfort Leroy, to let him know she was only there to help, but Steve didn't give her a chance. "Mrs. Hastings is not at her sister's, did not go there yesterday and never had plans to go."

"How do you know?" Leroy's bluster had begun to fade.

"Faye, her sister, told us. Now you tell us what really happened."

Leroy flung off his cap, ran blue-veined hands through his thinning hair and took a deep breath. "She was gone when I got home yesterday. There was a note." He studied the pink-flowered linoleum a moment before going on. "The note said she'd gone to Faye's."

"Where's the note?" Steve asked.

"Don't know. Trash can probably."

"Do you mind if we search the trash cans?" Steve asked politely. "That way we can confirm your story."

Leroy glowered at the young detective and bit his lip. "Oh, yeah. I remember now. I was mad. I crammed the note in my jacket pocket. I found it when I got to work today and tossed it there."

"Why were you mad?" Steve's voice was even, unhurried, as if the answer wasn't very important. Leroy made no answer. "Mr. Hastings," Steve asked again, "why were you mad?"

"Because she hadn't told me. Don't like her gallivanting off like that. She had no right to run off and leave me!"

Allison listened intently to the questions and answers. The Malvina she knew never *gallivanted* anywhere. And where, she wondered, was the sweet, devoted Leroy who'd been her neighbor for five years? She didn't recognize this angry, belligerent man who was accusing his wife of leaving him.

Steve sat in a chair opposite Leroy and leaned across the table so their faces were within inches of each other. "As I said before, Mr. Hastings, your wife did not go to Faye's. Is there any other place you think she may have gone? Other family? Friends?"

Leroy pulled back from the detective's accusing eyes. His voice faltered. "No. No family. Friends—but no one she'd spend the night with. I don't know where she could have gone. Or why."

Allison's feelings for Leroy bounced from suspicious to sympathetic. Had he harmed Malvina, or was he a deserted husband?

Steve continued his questions. "Did you have an argument? Some reason why she would want to leave?"

Leroy pushed back his chair, stumbled his way to the sink, filled a glass with water, and gulped it down before answering. His hostility returned. "No. We didn't have an argument. There was no reason for her to leave. I've always taken care of her. I always will." He turned to Allison. "You know. Haven't I always been here for her? Supported her? Paid her doctors' bills? Why would she leave?"

Allison shook her head, but before she could say anything Gil butted in. "Since you're so concerned about her, I'm sure you'll give us permission to search the house and your property. Right?"

The man's eyes blazed at the young officer. "Wrong. You don't need to be wasting your time here. The hospital. That's where you need to be looking. That's it. She may have had a bad spell and called an ambulance. You need to check the hospital."

Allison didn't say anything, but a red flag fluttered in her brain. He's lying, she thought. Surely he would already have called the hospital if, as he said, he came home yesterday and found her missing. And if he'd found a note, he probably would have called Faye.

Steve nodded. "Good idea. We'll check the hospital, and we'll check with the neighbors also. But first we want to search this house and grounds."

"Why? You've no right."

"We want to find your missing wife. Remember? If you don't agree, we can get a search warrant. It's up to you."

Leroy shrugged. "Go ahead. But you're not going to find anything here."

Steve gave instructions to the other officers. "Martha, suppose you and Gil look around in here, and Tim, you check outside. And while they're doing that, Mr. Hastings, let's go into the bedroom and you can tell me what clothes your wife took with her."

Steve took Leroy by the elbow and propelled him into the bedroom. Allison followed at a distance. She didn't want to get in the way, but neither did she want to miss anything. Steve opened the closet door, but Leroy refused to look. "How am I supposed to know? I don't pay attention to her clothes." Allison figured he was telling the truth in that statement, even if he had lied about everything else.

Martha came into the bedroom and Leroy wandered back into the kitchen. Steve motioned Allison to stay.

"Can you help us out, Mrs. Aldridge?" Steve asked. "Can you tell if any clothes are missing?"

"I'm afraid not. However, I did notice that her winter coat is gone. She hangs it on a hook by the kitchen door. It was hanging there when I was here on Monday. I don't see her go out often, but I assume she wears it when the weather is cold."

"Like today," Martha said, "and yesterday. You know, Steve, I have a bad feeling about this."

Steve nodded. "I know. Well, keep looking while I call the hospital and the cab company."

Allison followed Steve to the wall phone in the kitchen and unabashedly listened to his side of the conversation. It was obvious his inquiries received negative answers.

Leroy shed his outer coveralls and tossed them in a corner. He sat stooped over the kitchen table and cracked his grease-stained knuckles. Steve hunkered down across from him. "Got a recent picture of your wife?" Leroy gestured toward the desk and Steve flipped through a photo album. After a few moments he sighed. "Nothing much here."

"Just a minute," Allison said. "I remember Malvina showing me an anniversary portrait." She headed for the den and came back with a framed picture of Leroy and Malvina. It'd been taken a few years earlier when Malvina was still able to get out on her own. In the picture Malvina was smiling; Leroy looked like he was trying to.

"This will do," Steve said as he showed the picture to Leroy. "All right if we take it?"

Leroy didn't look up. "Suit yourself."

Tim came in, shaking cold rain from his cap. "I need a key to the storage shed. Everything else is clear."

Before Steve could ask him, Leroy pointed to the key rack by the phone. "It's hanging there. Help yourself, but I tell you, you're not going to find anything." Tim read the labels hanging on several keys, selected one and went back outside. He returned shortly and reported that he had found nothing unusual.

Gil came into the kitchen shaking his head. "Nothing, Sir. I've looked everywhere."

"What did I tell you?" Leroy bellowed. "Now maybe you'll get out and do some real searching for her."

Martha returned to the kitchen from the master bedroom. "Mr. Hastings, what time did your wife usually take her medications?"

"After breakfast, I think. Why?"

"Then I guess she didn't eat breakfast yesterday. Thursday's pills are still here, as are today's and Saturday's." Martha lifted up the seven-day pill dispenser. "Surely, she wouldn't have gone off visiting without taking her medicine with her."

"I don't know what's going on here, Mr. Hastings," Steve said, his voice harsh, "but I think you'd better come down to the station and make a complete statement."

"Are you arresting me just 'cause I don't know where my wife is?"

"No Sir. I'm not arresting you for anything. But I think it would be in your best interest to cooperate with our investigation."

SIX

ALLISON AWOKE EARLY the next morning without benefit of an alarm clock. On Saturdays she enjoyed the luxury of burrowing back under the covers or drinking coffee in bed or, if the weather was nice, a short jog around the block. Today, though, all she could think about were her neighbors. Leroy still hadn't gotten home by the time she had gone to bed last night, but now his car was in the drive. Her first thought was to go over and offer food and solace. On second thought, she decided she didn't want to confront the angry man she remembered from the previous evening.

Allison's questions and feelings tumbled over each other in her mind. Had Leroy harmed Malvina? Had she run away? If so, how had she left, and where had she gone? Steve had checked with the town's one cab company, and they hadn't picked her up. Faye could offer no possible explanation of why her sister would leave or where she might be. None of Malvina's heart medicines were gone. How long could she survive without them? Did any of the other neighbors have information, see anything unusual? And what had Malvina wanted to tell her that was so important?

She went through her usual motions of Saturday morning housecleaning. She vacuumed, dusted, piled newspapers in the recycling bin, changed the kitty litter. It didn't take long now that the children weren't here to mess up the house as soon as she'd cleaned.

It was a small house, which had been listed as a "starter home" when she'd bought it, but it'd been just right for her and the kids. Connie and Dave had loved having their own rooms after being in a cramped apartment. The backyard was perfect for softball practice, croquet, and running through the sprinkler on hot summer days. The house had proved to her that she could make it as a single mom. And somewhere along the line, it had restored her self-respect and self-confidence.

The kids had suggested she might want to sell the house now since they were practically on their own. Connie was in her senior year and would be entering med school soon. Dave still had two years of college and didn't know exactly what he would do next, but Allison sensed he wouldn't be returning to Holliston. The world was too big and too enticing for him to stay in the small town.

"You could get a nice condo and not have to worry about mowing the yard or raking leaves or repairing the furnace," Dave had said. She'd told him she would think about it. And she had. But not now, she'd concluded—not as long as she could take care of things. She and Lancelot were doing fine right here.

When she was taking the cat's litter pan out, she noticed Leroy's car was gone. At the same time she noticed a patrol car across the street and saw Tim going from house to house. The ice was melting quickly, and the morning held promise of a nice day. The sun had come out so brightly it seemed to be asking forgiveness for its recent absenteeism. Even so, Allison could not dismiss from her mind the dark cloud which seemed to envelope the neighborhood.

Steve drove up as Allison was finishing her fourth cup of coffee. She went to the carport and waved him in. "You okay?" he asked, concern evident in his voice and eyes.

"No. I'm not okay, not as long as Malvina is out there somewhere, and we don't know what's happening to her. Have you found out anything?"

"Not really. Leroy is sticking by his story. He came home, found her gone and found the note. And he doesn't know where she is."

"Do you believe him?"

"I'm not sure." Steve pointed toward the coffeepot. "Got any left?"

Allison nodded and poured him a cup. "You're not sure? What kind of answer is that?"

"The best I can do right now." Steve pulled out a kitchen chair, turned it around and straddled it. Allison had never figured out why men liked to do that. Was it reminiscent of pioneer days when they straddled a horse and rode off into the sunset? Or was it so they could rest their arms on the back of the chair while they pondered the mysteries of life? Steve certainly had a mystery to ponder here, so she didn't begrudge him this little comfort if it would help any.

"I almost believe the part about him not knowing where Malvina is," he said. "At this point I can't buy Gil's theory that he killed and buried her. But I also think he knows something he's not telling us. He may suspect who's involved and why Malvina was a target."

"A target? For what?"

Steve shrugged. "Information maybe. Leverage to get to him."

"It seems so unreal. Malvina wouldn't be involved in anything underhanded or crooked. She's just a nice person who cares only for her home and her husband. She has a bad heart, but she's accepted it and has done the best she could. I don't know why anybody would want to hurt her." Allison offered Steve a chocolate-covered donut and took one herself. "And what could anyone have against Leroy? None of it makes any sense."

"Tell me again about the last time you saw Malvina and what was said."

Allison retold about her visit on Monday afternoon, about their discussions, about Malvina giving her the calendar. "She was perfectly normal that day, and I remember she was excited when she told me Leroy had promised they'd take a vacation cruise this summer."

Steve crinkled his forehead in puzzlement and pulled

on his right ear lobe. "A cruise? How does a maintenance man afford a cruise? Rufus Crandall, the owner
of Valley Textiles, isn't known for his generosity to
employees. My granddad worked there for years and
the biggest bonus old man Crandall ever gave out was
a Christmas ham. Of course, he doesn't stint on his
own benefits. He's always taking what he refers to as,
'exploratory business trips.' Supposedly, he's looking
for places to expand, but I imagine the trips are really
vacations written off as business expenses."

"That's right," Allison said. "I remember a newspaper write-up last summer telling about his trips to
Mexico looking for product outlets. And it isn't likely
that Leroy would qualify for a business trip with the big
boss."

"So where was he planning on getting the money?"

"I guess he could have been saving for years."
Allison frowned. "But that hardly seems possible with
all of Malvina's medical expenses. I didn't think about
the cost when she was telling me. I was just happy for
her."

"So, anyway," Steve said, "the last time you know
for sure she was home was Monday afternoon. Right?"

Allison shook her head. "No. That was the last time
I saw her, but I know she was home Tuesday, Wednesday and Thursday mornings."

"How do you know that?"

"Because Leroy honked."

"He honked? Can you explain that a little more?"

"He always honked goodbye to her as he drove out to work. I thought it was so sweet of him. I imagined it was his way of telling her he'd be thinking of her while he was gone." Allison smiled at Steve who rolled his eyes toward the ceiling. "Do you think maybe I romanticized it too much?" Allison asked.

"Yes, I'd say you did. And how do you know he was honking on those days to really say goodbye? He could have been doing it to let you think his wife was still at home. She may have been missing for days as far as we know."

"That's where you're wrong, Steve. I know she was home Wednesday because she called and left a message on my answering machine. And remember, her medication had been taken through Wednesday." Allison closed her eyes and pursed her lips. It helped her think. "But you may be right about Thursday. She didn't take her medicine that day. In fact, she may have been gone Wednesday night when I called, and Leroy told me she was already in bed and asleep."

"Leroy knows more than he's telling, that's for sure." Steve gulped the rest of his coffee and stood up to leave.

"You'll keep me informed?" Allison said.

"You know I will. And if you think of anything else, call me. I may drop back by later tonight."

"Oh," Allison said, "I forgot to tell you. I won't be home this evening. I'm one of the hostesses at the art show tonight. You know, it's held every year at the library so local artists can display their works." She grinned at Steve. "Come to think of it, I've never seen you there. Why don't you drop in? Maybe a little culture will rub off on you."

"I may just do that, teacher, if you think it won't be too big of a shock to the artistic souls in town."

ALLISON ARRIVED AT the library early. She was putting out the punch bowl and cups when the other committee members came in. She had hoped the activity would allow her to banish Malvina from her thoughts, at least temporarily. No such luck. As in all small towns, good news traveled at the speed of light, and bad news surpassed even that. The gossip speeded up more when Clarisse, Allison's neighbor on the other side, traipsed in. After that, "Poor Malvina" started or ended every sentence as the ladies set up for the art show. The school break-in wasn't even mentioned, having been dismissed in most minds as a harmless prank.

Buck Franklin, acting as cashier again this year, set up his table near the exit. Buck was short, squat, big shouldered, and taciturn. His personality was a little on the blah side, but there was no doubt he was a patron of the arts, and he did his best to bolster sales at the show. There was no charge to view the exhibit, but every person who left without buying something received Buck's famous evil eye. The banner above his head boldly read, **Support Your Local Artists!** It was well known that after the show closed, Buck would wander around and buy up many of the unsold paintings to hang in his insurance office. He was one man who certainly put his money where his mouth was.

The usual assortment of art patrons began to trickle in shortly after seven. There were club ladies, members of the city council, art teachers who encouraged talented students, students who had been promised extra credit, and a handful of backyard artists who aspired to greater things. Any resident was eligible to submit entries, but not all submissions passed the final judgment of the Art Council.

Mr. Forster came in close to eight, wandered around with both hands behind his back, nodded approval of several works, greeted people with a cautious smile. When students saw him approaching, they put on faces of intense concentration. Allison knew the principal was not much of an art lover, but she appreciated his support of the show. Many of the other ladies in the Arts Council vied to show their appreciation as well.

The school principal, if not a fantastically eligible bachelor, was at least a bachelor; thus he always had a number of lonely widows and single ladies around him at public events. They chatted with him, smothered him with attention, tossed out veiled invitations.

Allison noticed that even Lorraine, whose husband hadn't been dead much over six months, fawned over him as he made his way past the refreshment table. "You must try one of my seafoam cookies," she said. "You'll never find anything like these in the grocery stores. It's a recipe my mother used for years." Mr.

Forster took one of the proffered delicacies, munched thoughtfully and nodded his approval. Lorraine beamed. "I'm so glad you could join us tonight. We seldom see you at any of the local functions anymore. You're away so often on weekends."

Mr. Forster wiped his lips on a napkin, took a sip of punch, and opened his mouth as if to respond, but Lorraine went blithely on, "Of course, I know how lonely weekends can be. I especially miss cooking a big Sunday dinner. It's no fun cooking for just one person. Don't you find Sunday afternoons simply drag by when you're all alone?"

Allison enjoyed Mr. Forster's discomfort and wondered how he was going to extricate himself from the situation when another one of the ladies came up to Lorraine with a message. "Buck needs your help at the sales table."

"Please excuse me," Lorraine said to the principal. "Duty calls. Help yourself to another cookie. I'll be right back."

He gave her a slight nod and as soon as her back was turned, he left the refreshment table to mingle with the crowd.

More people started streaming in, and Allison was busy at the punch bowl. During a break in the line, she glanced up and saw an elderly gentleman come in. He looked a little confused as to which way to go first. Allison asked Clarisse to take over for a few minutes, and headed in his direction. "Good evening, Professor

Keyes. It's so good to see you. May I help you off with your coat?"

"Yes, thank you." He slipped off his heavy black overcoat and squinted up at her. "Excuse me. I should know you, but the name eludes me. I don't get out much now I've retired."

"Allison Aldridge. I'm a teacher at Madison. You were kind enough to give my students a lecture once on medicinal herbs. They were very impressed that a college professor of botany would visit our classroom."

His frosty-white mustache drooped over smiling lips. "Yes. I recall now. One of your young men wanted to know if eating ginseng would improve his test scores."

Allison laughed. "He was willing to try anything except studying."

She led the professor to the start of the exhibit. "Take your time looking around and if you find anything you want to buy, someone will carry it out for you. And come over to get some refreshments before you leave."

"I'll do that."

Allison's gaze lingered on the old man. He reminded her of a picture of Mark Twain, the same bushy eyebrows and mustache, the same flowing white hair. Even the same subtle sense of humor. The college had lost a fine teacher when Professor Donald Keyes left. She hoped he would have many good years to enjoy his leisure time. He certainly deserved them. But, as Malvina's face popped up in her brain, she was reminded about how cruel Fate could sometimes be.

SEVEN

SHE MADE HER WAY BACK to the refreshment table, but Clarisse waved her off. "I'm doing fine here. You take a break and look around." Allison was always amazed at the variety and quality of the selected paintings, sketches and sculptures. The artists, having been assigned individual spaces, had set up their displays earlier, but Allison hadn't had a chance to study them. Now she joined the promenade around the exhibit hall, echoed the "Ohs" and "Ahs," the smiles, and the quizzical looks. She read each artist's name and recognized several of them. She paused before a watercolor of a rippling stream, vibrant fall leaves, and soft distant hills. It was titled, *Peace in the Valley*. It was the kind of painting Malvina would like, she thought. Allison hurried on. She didn't want to think about her missing neighbor right now; it was just too painful.

She continued her rounds looking for just the right picture to buy for her den. She was studying a sketch of a lonely railroad track with a distant steam locomotive when a voice interrupted her thoughts. "Makes me want to get on that train and ride forever. What do you think about it, Mrs. Aldridge?" She turned to meet a familiar face.

It took a few seconds for the face to register as a former student. "Wally. Wally Stitson. How nice to see you. It's been a while."

"Yeah. Sure has. You still at Madison?" His voice was soft, polite, as she remembered it from his school days. His appearance hadn't changed much either. His straggly dirt-brown hair fell from a middle part to mesh with thick eyebrows and lashes.

Allison recalled the many times she had instructed him to, "get your hair out of your eyes," and had a sudden urge to say it again. Instead she smiled and replied, "Surely am. And I remember you liked to sit in the back row drawing pictures when you should have been learning about strong bodies and bones."

"Oh, but I did learn about bones—and made a profit on it. My pictures of skeletons sold for a dime each."

Allison laughed. "About those skeletons—they seemed to have a few extra appendages in rather inappropriate places."

"Nothing wrong with trying to improve on nature." Wally grinned, but the smile didn't reach his eyes. Allison remembered him as never really fitting in. He was smart and talented, but he didn't seem to have any close buddies. He went out for a few sports but spent most of his time on the bench. She recalled encouraging him at one time to do some sketches for the art show, but he'd shaken his head. "That's kid stuff," he'd said. "When I'm ready, I'll show people what a real artist can do."

"So," she asked him, "are you still drawing pictures?"

"Now and then. Actually, I'm getting pretty good."

"I'm glad to hear it. I'd love to see some of your work."

"That might just happen." Wally gave her a half-smile and glanced at his watch. "But I've got to be going soon." He turned and hesitated. "If you're ready to leave, I'll walk you to your car."

"Thanks, but I'll be here until the last straggler leaves, and then I have to help with the clean up."

"Well, have a nice evening. 'Bye."

He was gone before Allison could say anything else. She watched him grab a black jacket from where it hung by the door and hurry out. I wonder what kind of art he's doing, she thought. It'd be nice if he could make a success of it.

The crowd had dwindled considerably when Steve meandered in. He'd changed from suit and tie to casual slacks and a denim jacket. He wandered around the room, but Allison noticed he was studying the people more than the art works. It would take more than a change of clothes, she mused, to stifle his sleuthing instincts.

He greeted her and the other ladies, but made no mention of the thing that was uppermost in their minds. Clarisse wasn't going to let him get away with that. She clutched his arm and hissed. "Do tell me you've some word on poor Malvina. We're all just worried sick about her."

Steve shook his head and extricated his limb. "Sorry. Nothing to report." He nodded to the assembled group and quickly fled the scene.

ALLISON WAS ABLE TO LEAVE the art show sooner than she expected. Clarisse volunteered for clean-up duty and urged Allison to go home. "You look like you need a good night's rest. Scoot now and I'll finish up here."

Allison didn't argue. She gathered her coat, her handbag, and the splash of framed color she had purchased titled, *Breakthrough.* The artist had classified it as postmodern optical art. Allison was a traditionalist, but decided maybe it was time to expand her artistic horizons. It would be a marvelous conversation piece with its geometric figures, the wild colors, and perhaps hidden symbolism.

It was only a little after nine o'clock when she drove into her carport. The porch light welcomed her home. The wind picked up as she toted the painting from the backseat. She shivered, hurriedly found her key, and opened the door. The expected warmth reached out and hugged her as she shed her gray wool coat, turned on the kitchen light, and headed for the hall closet. She hung up her coat and parked the painting in the back of the closet. The sound of the whistling wind echoed as if determined to dispel the coziness of the house.

Allison glanced at the beckoning red dot on the answering machine and hoped it would be Fred. He usually called a couple of times a week and they would catch up on each other's lives. His was as exciting as hers was dull, but this week it would be different. She would tell him about the school break-in and about the terrible news of Malvina's disappearance. Not that he could do anything about either one, but it would be good to have a sympathetic ear.

She plopped down in the recliner and without bothering to turn the den light on, she pushed the button and smiled at her friend's voice. "And where is my favorite girl tonight? Call me when you get in, if you're not too exhausted from your busy social life."

Allison sighed. She wished Fred lived closer. He seemed so far away, even though it was only a few hours drive. It wasn't easy to build a relationship over the phone. She wasn't even sure it was a relationship they were building. They enjoyed chatting, they shared much the same values and they were both lonely, but would it ever go any further than that? He was a bachelor in his fifties and she was a divorcee in her forties. They both had careers they loved, although Fred had hinted that he was thinking about retiring from his county police department. He'd spent Christmas with her and her kids. He'd seemed to enjoy them and they'd thoroughly approved of him. But now it was back to just phone calls, and Allison wondered if the calls were enough.

The kitchen light gave her just enough illumination to dial his number. She enjoyed sitting in the near darkness while they talked. It made her feel closer to him. He picked up on the first ring. Good, she thought, he was waiting for her call.

After the preliminary "Hellos" and light banter, Allison plunged into the tales of the school break-in and her missing neighbor. She got as far as, "And Malvina hasn't been seen or heard from since Thursday. I'm afraid something terrible has happened to her." A cold gust of wind sent a chill through Allison and rattled a hanging chime above the mantle. "Just a minute, Fred," she said, "there's a terrible draft in here. Must be coming from the fireplace. Hang on while I check it."

Allison laid down the phone and switched on the lamp. She scanned the room—and screamed!

EIGHT

FRED HEARD THE SCREAM and felt helpless. Allison was in trouble and there wasn't a thing he could do. He wanted to call out to her, demand she pick up the phone, beg her to speak to him. At the same time, his detective mind told him to be quiet, to listen. If someone else was in the room, he wanted to hear what was said, what was done. But there was nothing, no more screams, no other voice. Then he heard a soft sobbing. He'd never heard Allison cry before, and the sound tore at his heart.

After what seemed like a lifetime, Fred heard the phone scratching against a surface and then Allison's voice, low and scared. "He was here. He came here just like I was afraid he would. Steve had new locks installed, but he still got in."

Chilling questions teased Fred's mind. Who was *he,* and who was Steve, and was he still there, and was Allison in danger? Fred knew his questions would have to wait. Allison's safety was his first concern. "Allison," he commanded, "hang up and call 9-1-1. Now! Stay on the phone with them until help gets there. Then call me back." Allison grunted and Fred heard the phone click. "And be careful," he said to the buzz of the dial tone.

Fred had been attracted to Allison the first time he'd met her at the Blue Goose Lodge the previous summer. He liked her curiosity, her quick mind, and her even quicker laughter. Her inquisitive nature, or what some would call her snooping instinct, helped solve the murder he was investigating. But what he admired most was her gutsy approach to life. She'd reared two kids on her own, could laugh at her own foibles, would stick her neck out for a friend—or for a stray cat.

He'd come to care for Allison a great deal, but he hadn't realized just how much he cared until he heard that awful scream. He clenched his hands and stared at the phone. How long before it would ring and assure him of her safety? He wouldn't allow his mind to think of any other outcome.

ALLISON SENT UP a silent prayer as she dialed the emergency number, then did her best to control the tremor in her voice as she described her situation. "Someone broke into my home. The patio door is shattered. It's a mess everywhere." The voice on the other end of the line was calm and professional. It helped slow her pounding pulse. Allison managed to give her name and address, but her throat squeezed shut as she strangled out, "Help me."

"Someone is on the way," the calm voice said. "They'll be there shortly. Are you alone?"

"Yes. I think so." Allison's eyes searched the room, skimming over the scattered books and pictures and papers to the dark corners, to the drawn drapes, to her open bedroom door. "I don't hear anybody," she said, her voice barely a whisper. "He must be gone."

Another gust of wind pushed its way through the broken glass and danced with the chimes. In the midst of their tinkling, Allison thought she detected an added sound. A faint squeak? Footsteps? She held her breath.

The voice on the phone interrupted Allison's concentration. "Just stay on the line. Officers are on the way."

There it was again—from the hallway—the wind? A step? Allison could feel her heart galloping, the hand that held the phone became damp with sweat. She tried to take a deep breath to calm her rising panic but could only come out with quick gasps.

Now there was no mistake. There was a noise coming from the basement. She stared at the basement door. The bolt that she had kept carefully closed was open. Someone was down there. And he must have heard her come in. Could she cover the few feet to the door, slide the bolt, trap her intruder? She rose slowly, silently from her chair, the phone still to her ear. But before she had a chance to move farther, the basement door creaked open. A black figure loomed in the hallway.

Allison covered her mouth to smother the coming scream. Her eyes probed the shadows. Black gloved hands emerged—hands holding a bat!

The voice in her ear continued, "Just stay on the line, stay calm and someone will be there soon."

Soon isn't soon enough, Allison thought wildly. "Oh, God," she cried, "I need help NOW!" She pitched the cordless phone at the approaching figure, heard a snarled curse and, without looking back, fled to her bedroom. She slammed the door shut, leaned against it, tried to catch her breath. Her hands were trembling; the room seemed to be spinning; her legs wobbled. She closed her eyes, prayed for calmness.

Her breathing slowed, and she heard footsteps coming toward the door. She positioned her right shoulder against a chest of drawers, shoved with all her strength, and managed to maneuver it in front of the knob. She knew it was only a delaying tactic. Anyone determined to get in would get in. She tore into the bathroom and snapped the lock.

Then she crouched on the commode, covered her face, and wailed long and loud.

In a few moments, however, her common sense kicked in. Allison stopped crying and listened. She held her breath and strained to hear if there was the slightest movement outside her sanctuary. All was quiet. She didn't dare move or open the door. After a couple of minutes she started breathing normally and her fear subsided to a manageable level.

Then her ears again picked up other sounds: a slamming car door, a knock, a familiar voice. "Mrs. Aldridge, it's Tim McCall. Are you all right?" Relief washed over her. Now she knew how besieged pioneers felt when they heard the cavalry riding to their rescue.

She flipped the bathroom door lock, ran to the chest of drawers, started pushing. It was harder moving it away from the door than getting it there. Allison guessed her supply of adrenalin was completely depleted. She made one final thrust and was able to open the door enough to squeeze through. Allison made it to the kitchen just in time to save the door from being kicked in. "Oh, am I glad to see you." She let in the two officers she'd met at Malvina's the night before.

"Are you all right?" Tim asked again as his eyes roamed the room.

"I guess so. I'll let you know as soon as my heart starts beating again."

Martha pushed in behind Tim, wrapped an arm around Allison and led her to a chair. "Now you just sit there and get control of yourself while we look around." Martha grabbed a jacket from a hook by the door and draped it over Allison's shoulders. "Give us a few minutes. We'll be right back."

Tim and Martha made a quick tour of the house, including the basement, and returned to the kitchen. Tim reported to Allison. "Whoever it was is gone now." He had picked up the phone where it lay in the hallway and shook it in front of her face. "Mrs. Aldridge, why is the phone on the floor? You were supposed to stay on the line until we got here."

Allison didn't like Tim's scolding tone of voice.

"Well, I would have if you'd gotten here sooner. But since my intruder was coming at me with a weapon, I decided to hit and run. You only missed him by a couple of minutes."

"You saw him?" Tim asked. "Can you give us a description? What kind of weapon? What happened? Did he hurt you?"

Allison felt close to tears again, but she didn't want to break down in front of the officers. She headed for the cabinets. "I think I need some coffee."

"You go ahead," Martha said. "Relax a little. Then we'll get to the details."

Allison hadn't paid a lot of attention to either of the officers the evening before at the Hastings' house. Now she did. Martha was small in stature, short permed hair— pale blond, pleasant but plain features, and a wedding ring on the proper finger. "I should know you," Allison said, "but I don't think you were a student of mine."

"No. I went to Prince Academy. But I did go to your church. You probably know my parents. My maiden name was Pickney."

"Of course. You used to sing in the youth choir."

"That's right. Seems like I don't have much time for church anymore, though."

"But she still sings," Tim said. "You should have heard her when we went caroling at the homeless shelter before Christmas. She brought the house down."

"And you made a Santa those men will never forget," Martha said.

Tim grinned, shrugged his football shoulders and rubbed reddish bristles appearing on his chin. "Must have been the red beard. But I guess we'd better get back to the business at hand." He turned to Allison. "Can you give us any kind of description?"

Allison shook her head, but before she could say anything, the kitchen door banged open and Gil breezed into the room. He was bareheaded and wore a black and gold high school letter jacket. "Heard the news on my scanner," he announced. "My night off, but I thought y'all might need some help."

Tim smiled. Martha didn't. "I think we can handle everything," she said. "And you can go back home like a good little boy and play with your toys."

"Don't pay any attention to her, Gil," Tim said. "She had a little barbed wire mixed in with her salad tonight. Stick around and we'll put you to work."

Tim looked at the phone he still held in his hand and replaced it in its base. It rang immediately. Allison jumped. "That must be Fred. I was supposed to call him back."

Tim stepped back as Allison snatched the phone. "Yes?…Yes, I'm okay, Fred…The police are here. Someone broke in. I don't know yet what's missing… All right. Hold on." Allison held the phone out. "He wants to talk to one of you."

Tim looked at her warily. "Who is it?"

"A friend of mine, Fred Sawyer. He's a police officer, too. I was talking to him when I realized there had been a break-in." Tim frowned. Allison decided he looked like a kid who thought he must have done something wrong, but couldn't figure out what. "Go ahead." She laughed. "He's not going to bite you."

Tim still hesitated and Gil took the phone. "Watts here." Allison surveyed the havoc in the den while Gil reassured Fred everything was under control. "Yes sir. I'll see to it…Yes sir, we'll report back as soon as we're finished…Yes sir." Gil dropped the phone in Allison's hand. "For heaven's sake, convince him you're all right, so we can get on with the investigation."

When Allison hung up, Gil laughed nervously, "I didn't know you had such big shot friends."

Allison smiled. She felt no compulsion to explain that Fred was no big shot, just a very dear friend.

"Let that be a lesson to you, Sonny," Martha said. "A lot of us have friends in high places."

Gil gave her a dirty look and turned to Tim. His voice was respectful as he asked, "What do you want me to do?"

Allison looked from Martha to Gil and wondered why Martha was being so rude to him. But whatever the problem between the two, she didn't have time to think about it now. She had to try to make sense of what had happened in her house.

The investigation revealed little. The intruder had gained entrance by smashing the glass of the patio door with a rock. The hole in the door was big enough to allow a hand to reach through and dislodge the protective bar. Allison decided she needed to have a little talk with Steve about his security devices. Of course, he may not have realized how old the door was. She knew that most patio doors today would be made of shatter-proof glass.

The rock was found on the carpet and was now tagged as evidence. A fat lot of good that will do, she thought, there are dozens more just like it in the flower bed.

The intruder had rifled through desks, bookcases, drawers, flipped through books and magazines, emptied trash cans. He made no effort to be neat as he had at the school. When he'd finished all the first floor rooms, he'd gone downstairs and ransacked the recreation room. That was when Allison had come home.

She remembered the gloved hand holding the bat, so obviously there would be no fingerprints. Gil brought in the bat that had been dropped in the yard. "Recognize this?" he asked Allison.

She nodded. "That's what he was holding. It belongs to my son, Dave." Allison shuddered as she realized how close the intruder had been to her. "I must have come home earlier than he expected and when he heard me call for help, he knew he had to get out."

"But who knew you'd be away tonight?" Gil asked.

Allison wrinkled her nose in thought. "Lots of people. I help out with the art show every year so all the people associated with that would have known. Or someone could have been watching and saw me drive out. And, of course, the police knew. I told Steve this morning. That makes for rather a broad field of suspects, doesn't it?"

Tim dropped down on the couch and stared at his notes. Allison suspected he wasn't yet comfortable with being an officer in charge. He looked up at her. "You didn't get even a glimpse at his face?"

"No," Allison said. "All I could see was the bat in his hands. I think he was dressed all in black." Allison stared at the hallway where the intruder had been. "Well, maybe I did see his face for a moment, but either it was in the shadows or he had on a dark mask. All I remember is something dark."

"A ski mask, maybe?" Martha asked. Martha hadn't said much during their search, but Allison sensed she was taking in every bit of information. "Let's try an experiment," she now suggested. "Allison, fix the lights the way they were and then, Gil, you come out from the basement door and let's see if Allison can identify you."

"Why me?" Gil flared. "You take the bat and do it yourself."

Without a word, Martha grabbed the bat, opened the basement door and closed it after herself. Allison turned off all the lights except the one in the kitchen and the lamp by the phone. The basement door slowly opened, the end of the bat appeared, a hand appeared and Martha's face appeared. "There's enough light to make out your face, Martha," Allison said. "So he must have had some kind of mask on."

"Not that it helps much to know," Martha conceded. "A man could have been wearing a ski mask but had the front pulled up like a stocking cap. On a cold night like this, it wouldn't have attracted any attention. He probably lowered the mask when he came up the stairs so you couldn't see his face."

"Right," Allison said. "But he must have walked from somewhere because I didn't notice a strange car parked in the area when I came home. Someone may have noticed him even if he didn't look suspicious at the time."

Tim nodded. "We'll check with the neighbors in the morning. And look for footprints. We might be able to get some good ones since the snow and ice have melted and left plenty of mud."

"Speaking of neighbors," Allison said, "Leroy's car has been gone since this morning. Did he have permission to leave town?"

"We didn't have enough to charge him with anything." Martha was taking more pictures but wasn't missing a beat of the conversation. "He may have gone off to look for Malvina himself."

"Or to make sure the body was well buried," Gil added.

Allison looked from one to the other and to the chaos surrounding her. "Do you think there's a connection? Could Malvina's disappearance have anything to do with the break-ins?"

"There's a connection," Tim said. "I have no idea

what it is, but they're all tied together with the same black thread."

Gil turned to Allison, "And you still say you don't know what our friend was looking for?"

"Gil Watts," Allison said, "if I knew what he wanted, I'd hand it to him on a silver platter. I just want an end to all this crazy business and for Malvina to be home safely. I tell you I have absolutely nothing of value in this house." Allison swiped away angry tears. "I don't understand what's happening to my life, to our town. This has always been such a peaceful valley."

NINE

TIM SUGGESTED THAT Allison spend the night at a local motel. It was fine with her. She didn't expect to sleep much, no matter where she laid her head. She packed her overnight bag and picked out a dress for church in the morning. As she was doing so, she realized she hadn't seen Lancelot since she'd come in. But she knew exactly where to look for the elusive cat.

She got down on her knees, pulled back the dust ruffle on her bed and peered into the darkness. Two shiny, scared feline eyes stared back. "It's okay, Lancelot," she crooned. "The bad man is gone. You can come out now." The cat wasn't so easily convinced since there were still strange voices coming from the den. Allison's hand clawed under the bed, caught a handful of orange neck fur and hauled Lancelot out. She cradled the cat in her left arm and stroked him lightly. "Did that mean old man scare you? Well, don't worry. We're going to catch him soon, and then he won't bother anybody ever again." Lancelot started purring at the reassuring words. Allison wished she could convince herself of that last statement as easily as she had her cat. "I can't take you with me now," she explained, "but you'll be fine until I get back tomorrow." She felt the cat understood and believed her. He gave one last purr and retreated back under the bed.

Tim called Steve who instructed him to leave everything undisturbed. Tim explained to Allison, "He'll be out first thing in the morning. No need for him to come tonight. He agreed you should go to a motel and just leave everything as it is."

Martha, however, insisted on doing one thing before they left. "We've got to tape something over the hole in the patio door." She picked up a Newsweek magazine, found some masking tape on the desk and handed both to Gil. "Here, make yourself useful. The furnace will run all night if we don't block out that cold wind. And you know what that'll do to her electric bill."

Gil gave her a wicked grin. "Now, how would I know that? Seeing as how I was brought up in a tar paper shack with no electricity."

"Sure," Martha said, "and no running water and you had to run barefoot through the snow to the outhouse and Santa Claus was never able to find your house. I've heard it all before. Quit whining and get to work fixing that hole."

Allison studied the two officers. Both wore tight smiles, but she wondered if some real conflict was cloaked by their light banter. Allison knew Martha's upbringing, the guidance and values she'd been given. But there was hardness in her voice now that Allison had difficulty assessing. On the other hand, Allison knew nothing of Gil's background. Maybe he did have a rough start in life, but why should that be an issue now?

"That should keep out Old Man Frost as well as the bogeyman," Gil said as he gave a last swirl with the tape.

"Good." Tim nodded approval. "Thanks for your help, Gil. I appreciate you coming over on your night off." Tim gave him a smile. "You're a good man, Charlie Brown."

"No problem." Gil appeared a little embarrassed by the compliment.

"Well, let's get out of here," Tim said. "Martha and I will follow you to the motel. I'll have the night patrol team swing by here and keep a close watch. We'll continue the investigation in the morning."

The only flaw in that plan was the unexpected rain at daybreak. It washed away any footprints the intruder might have left in the yard. Martha had taken photographs of the ground adjacent to the patio, but they showed no identifiable footprints.

ALLISON RECEIVED two morning calls at the motel. The first was from Steve. "Gil and I are heading to your house now. Tim left the key you gave him, so I'll let myself in. Gil will fill me in, and then I need to talk to you. Can you come home in a couple of hours?"

Allison hesitated. "I guess so. But I was planning to go to church." Her voice quivered. "Steve, I need to go to church—today of all days." Allison knew God was with her anytime and anywhere, but she always felt closer to Him in church and when she was by the ocean. The ocean was too far to go today.

"I understand," Steve said. "Come home as soon as church is over. We'll be here. How about if I bring some KFC? We can talk over Sunday dinner, and brag about what good cooks we are."

Allison laughed. "You've never eaten my cooking, or you wouldn't ever accuse me of bragging. I'll see you then."

The second caller was Fred. She'd called him back the night before after she'd gotten to the motel. At that time he'd made no mention of coming to check on her, and she went to sleep wondering if he was really concerned about her. This morning when she answered the phone, his voice came booming over the line. "I'm leaving now. I'll be at your house in a few hours."

Allison bristled at his commanding tone. He could at least have asked how she was feeling, or if she'd gotten any sleep. Did he think he could just ride in on his white horse and she would swoon in relief?

Allison's response was cool. "That's not necessary. We have a very competent police force here."

"They don't sound very competent to me if they can't prevent break-ins or find missing people."

Silence weighed heavily on the telephone line between the two friends. Allison knew Fred was upset, but he had no right to barge into her life and her town with the intent of taking over.

Fred must have realized Allison had misunderstood his concern. "Hey, I'm sorry," he said. "It's just that I've been so doggone worried about you. I want to be sure you're okay." He paused just long enough for his contrition to invade Allison's heart. "May I come up?"

She was glad Fred couldn't see her self-satisfied smile. "Of course, you may. I'd be delighted if you'd come for lunch—chicken and fixin's." Actually she was thrilled he was coming, but for some perverse reason she hesitated to let him know that.

When she was around Fred, she always felt warm and safe. On the other hand, her years of self-reliance, of raising her kids alone, of having no one else around, had made her wary of letting down her defenses. Maybe it was something she needed to work on.

ALL THE POLICE PEOPLE in Allison's crazy life were already at her home when she returned from church. Fred's steel-blue Camry was parked behind two patrol cars. Gil and Tim were examining the ground beyond the carport, Martha was halfway up the block knocking on doors. Looking through the kitchen window, Allison could see Steve and Fred talking animatedly. Good, Allison thought, they must have made their own introductions. She was a little uneasy, though. What if Fred tried to interfere in a police investigation where he had absolutely no jurisdiction? And she wondered if Gil still considered Fred a big shot.

Fred greeted Allison with a light peck on the cheek and she gave him a shy smile. Even though they had spent Christmas Day together, it seemed like months instead of weeks since she'd seen him. She was glad she'd worn her lavender blue dress that morning. It made her feel pretty and feminine. Fred had on jeans and a bright yellow knit shirt. He looked like a ray of sunshine. "I'm glad you came," she whispered.

"Me too," he murmured back.

Steve grinned at the two of them. "I've been filling your boyfriend in on what we know, Mrs. Aldridge. It's always good to get outside opinions."

Allison blushed at the mention of boyfriend, but re-covered quickly enough to say, "And Fred always has an opinion to offer."

"And my opinion right now," Fred said, "is that we ought to eat while we talk. Chicken has a way of stimu-lating my brain cells."

Allison set out a pile of plates while Steve gave a holler to the men outside. "Martha should be working her way back down the street soon," he said. "But as my mama used to say, 'Time nor tide nor chicken tarrieth for no man.'"

Fred reached for a drumstick. "Your mama was a wise woman."

Gil and Tim came in the house, washed up at the sink and wasted no time in filling their plates. The men were all happily chowing down before Allison could get her biscuit buttered. For the first time that weekend she felt hungry. "Now, you fellows can talk all you want to while you're eating, but don't dare ask me a question until I've had my fill."

The men nodded their agreement. They started by feeling each other out about basketball loyalties: the Bobcats versus the Bulls, Duke versus any other Southern college team, Michael Jordan's legacy versus any other living player. This naturally led to upcoming baseball spring training, the Braves' chances this year, and the planned increase in admission prices to baseball games.

"If prices go up much more," Tim said, "the average man won't have enough money to get inside a ballpark."

"Speaking of money," Fred said between bites of beans and slaw, "has any of the funny money floating around the South found its way to Holliston yet?"

Steve shook his head. "Not to my knowledge. Nothing has been reported, anyway. But I hear there's been a lot in Miami and Atlanta. Any your way?"

"Yeah, a couple of twenties at WalMart, and a Franklin showed up at a motel. Probably just the beginning."

Gil stopped his chewing long enough to comment, "I'd be suspicious of any hundred dollar bill at a motel. Everybody pays with credit cards now."

Martha had come in, reached for a plate and joined the conversation. "Unless you don't want your wife to know you were at a motel."

Gil grinned at her. "So that's why your hubby always pays in cash."

Allison saw Martha's lips tighten and her hand shake. The policewoman concentrated on finding just the right piece of chicken before she answered. "I have more important things to do than worry about what my hubby does."

Allison's heart went out to the young woman. Maybe Gil had just been joking, she thought, but she could see pain in Martha's eyes. Allison understood. She'd been told that passing years would lessen her own pain of betrayal. And it had, but there were still times when she wondered if she could ever completely trust another man.

Silence hovered over the table. Allison felt she had to say something, no matter how inane. "So, what about this funny money?"

Gil was quick to answer her. "It pops up every once in a while, you know. Mostly casual stuff."

"Casual?" Allison didn't know what he was talking about. "You mean, like, not serious?"

Fred jumped in. "Oh, they're serious, all right. Just not very good. Casual counterfeit bills have a flat look and feel, whereas genuine bills have a three-dimensional look."

"But they're good enough to fool people?" Allison forgot about eating as she became engrossed in the subject of funny money.

"Sure. Most people don't look closely at their

money." Fred cleared his throat and took a gulp of iced tea. "I even got stuck with a fake twenty last fall."

"You?" Allison sounded appalled. "Fred Sawyer, the great detective, whose office walls are covered with commendations? You got fooled with a phony bill?"

Martha giggled. Tim snickered. Gil snorted. Steve gave them all a dirty look. Allison figured he didn't want his team to show disrespect to another law enforcement officer.

It didn't seem to bother Fred as he explained, "Yeah, well, you see, it was at the county fair and our sheriff's department had a booth selling hot dogs to raise money for a local kid who needed a bone marrow transplant. We were so busy, who had time to check each bill? We raised over a thousand dollars."

"And, of course, you replaced the phony twenty out of your own pocket?" Gil asked, still chuckling at the thought of someone ripping off the law.

Fred grimaced. "You'd better believe it. The other fellows wouldn't let me off the hook." Even Steve couldn't resist laughing at the ribbing Fred must have taken.

When the giggling subsided, Allison returned to the point in question. "Let me get this straight," she said. "These casual counterfeits are easy to spot if you're looking for them, but ordinary people like me wouldn't suspect them?"

"That's right," Gil said. "We professionals can tell a fake just by its feel. That is, unless you're too busy slinging hot dogs."

Fred ignored Gil's last statement, but it irritated Allison. There's something about Gil's manner that rubs me the wrong way, she thought. Is it just me, or does he want to provoke others into snapping back at him? She wondered again about his background. Maybe he'd been reared in a climate of confrontation and hadn't been able to break the habit. Allison turned her back on Gil and concentrated on what Fred was saying.

"The interesting thing about this latest money," Fred said, directing his comments to Steve, "is that they're duplicating the old twenties and hundreds. The new style is too difficult to copy."

"Which is precisely why the treasury department made the new bills." Steve pushed his plate aside, reached in his shirt pocket and pulled out a pack of gum. He passed it around, but the only taker was Gil. "You trying to quit smoking, too?" Steve asked him.

"Heck no," Gil said, "but I figured if I tried to light one up in here, teacher would invite me to step outside."

"You're right about that," Allison said. "And you'd better not drop a butt in my yard either."

Martha gave Allison a thumbs-up and then turned to Fred. "But if they're making new old bills wouldn't they stand out? I mean, if the old design is on a new bill, it would be a dead giveaway."

"No. These guys aren't dumb. They wash the bills or do something to them so they look like they've been around for years. But what we've done in our depart-ment," Fred again turned to Steve, "and what you might want to try here, is to encourage your merchants to use the felt markers on all big bills."

Steve nodded. "Actually we've already done that. Passed the pens out to all the big stores, but not many bother to use them."

Again the conversation had lost Allison. "What felt markers?"

This time it was Martha who educated her. "They're special pens. When they're swiped across real money it leaves a different color streak than if it's counterfeit. The ones we gave out to our merchants streak yellow on good money. But if it smears black, then the money is fake. It's a reaction to the paper."

"Sounds simple enough," Allison said.

"It is," Steve agreed. "We just have to get people to use them."

"But," Allison asked, "aren't the old bills being retired when they're turned into the banks? Seems like there wouldn't be many of the old ones still in circulation."

"More than you might think," Steve said, "small businesses, hoarders, people who don't trust banks." He pushed back his chair, gave his gum a few good chews, and pulled out his notebook. "But enough of that. Let's get down to the real business we're here for. Who is our intruder, and is the same person responsible for the disappearance of Malvina Hastings?"

TEN

TRYING TO GET COMFORTABLE, Malvina stirred on the narrow cot. The afternoon sun pierced the drawn blinds, splashed across the worn linoleum, ricocheted into her tear-stained eyes. "I've got to sit up," she cried to the vacant room. "My feet are going asleep." She felt the dull ache in her chest mushroom to a sharp pain as she tried to slide her legs over the side of the cot. With her ankles strapped together, she had to maneuver them as one entity. Propping up on one elbow, she managed to heave her upper body to a sitting position. The rope on her wrists tightened and she could feel another layer of her soft skin peeling away as easily as a bruised peach. Biting her lips, Malvina forced back tears. She was determined not to cry anymore. It was just too painful to bring her hands up to wipe her eyes and nose.

When her captor had started to leave that morning, Malvina had begged him not to tie her up again. She should have saved her breath.

"As soon as I'm gone," he'd said, "you'll be out of here faster than a hound dog chasin' coons."

"Joe, be reasonable," she'd pleaded. "Where would I go? There's no houses around here. And I'm so weak

I can barely walk. You can lock the door, nail the windows shut, but please, not the rope."

He ignored her, just as he had ignored all her questions and pleadings for the past four days. Malvina knew that Joe wasn't his real name. He refused to tell her his name, or why he was kidnapping her, or how he knew Leroy, or what lay in store for her.

She'd been such a fool when she'd first listened to him. "I'm Joe Smith," he'd said, flashing her a boyish smile. "I'm a friend of Leroy's, and he asked me to do him a little favor."

Malvina sat on the side of the cot, stared at the faded orange blanket, tried to ease the taut rope on her wrists, and reviewed the past week.

HER NIGHTMARE HAD STARTED Monday evening. She'd been telling Leroy about Allison's visit that afternoon when he'd become very angry with her. She still really didn't understand why. It seemed like such a minor thing, giving Allison something that would have gone in the trash anyway.

Leroy had been testy the last few months, though, and little things upset him easily. She assumed it had to do with the rumors of the mill closing and moving to Mexico. It wouldn't be easy for a man nearing retirement age to find another job. She'd tried to reassure him. She kept reminding him that their needs were few, and it would be nice to have more time to spend together. A couple of weeks ago, he'd surprised her by agreeing with her. He'd even promised to take her on a cruise this summer. She hadn't questioned where the money would come from; she just felt relieved that Leroy seemed happier. That's why she'd been so taken aback by his angry outburst. "Get it back! You hear me? Just get it back. You had no right to give it away without asking me."

He'd slammed into the bedroom, and she could hear him on the phone but couldn't make out what was being said. Later that evening he'd apologized for yelling at her, and told her to forget all about it. She gladly did so.

She forgot about it, that is, until he'd called from work late Wednesday afternoon. His voice frightened her. It was low and sounded far away. "You've got to do it. Don't ask questions. Just get the calendar back from Allison."

He knew she'd do anything for him. But Allison hadn't been home when she'd called, and she'd left a message. Earlier that day Malvina had noticed some curious goings-on next door. Allison had come home mid-morning with a strange young man, then a locksmith van arrived. Now she wondered if there might be a connection between them and the calendar.

When Leroy had gotten home and she hadn't yet retrieved the calendar, he blew up again. She tried to calm him. "I'll call Allison again as soon as I see her car drive in."

But he'd been beyond calming. "Never mind," he yelled. "I'll take care of it myself. Don't you say a word to her or to anybody. Don't ever mention it as long as you live!" He'd upset her so, she started having chest pain. She stumbled to the bedroom, slipped a nitro tablet under her tongue, dropped on the bed, and sobbed. When the phone rang, she made no effort to answer it. She was sure it was Allison returning her call, and wondered what Leroy would tell her.

Later Leroy stuck his head in the door. "I'm sleeping in the spare bedroom. Don't bother to get my breakfast in the morning."

She made no answer. What could she say? She loved Leroy, but his manner was scaring her. What kind of trouble was he in? What kind of trouble was she in? She simply didn't understand what was going on.

Thursday morning she waited until she heard his car start and his goodbye honks before getting out of bed. She tried to go about her usual morning activities. She made up both beds, washed the dirty dishes, and watched the school bus swallow up the neighborhood children. One by one, cars up and down the street departed to offices, stores, factories. Her eyes stayed focused on Allison's drive long after her neighbor had gone, wondering what Leroy had meant when he said he'd take care of it himself.

She was about ready to eat her breakfast, when she noticed a black car drive slowly past their house and stop in front of Allison's. Not many people drive black cars anymore, she thought. Black now seemed reserved for new luxury cars or old clunkers. This one was of the old clunker variety.

A young man, whose faded black jeans and jacket, matched the car, slid out slowly. She watched him as he made his way around the carport to the rear of her neighbor's house. She could only see his back as he stepped onto Allison's patio and fumbled at the door. She debated a few seconds whether she should call out to him or call the police.

She opened the window. "Hey, you there. What do you think you're doing? Get away from there or I'll call the police."

He backed away from the door, took a good look at her, and his face lit up with a smile. "Oh, good morning, Mrs. Hastings. I'm Joe Smith. I'm a friend of Leroy's. Nothing to worry about. He asked me to do him a little favor. Mrs. Aldridge told him he could go in and pick up something of his. Leroy wanted me to get it for him."

"I don't believe you. You were breaking into her house."

"Hey, take it easy." The smile faded. "Let me explain." He started heading her way. "I'll come in and explain."

"You will not come in!" She slammed the window shut and hurried as fast as she could to the kitchen door. She knew Leroy never locked the door after himself. But Joe beat her to it, pushed his way in, and positioned himself between her and the phone.

"Now, there's nothing to get excited about. I was just trying to help Leroy." Malvina studied the young man. He was thin and pale, black gloved hands poised in front of him, black cap pulled far down on his forehead. "Maybe he didn't tell you, but he's in big trouble."

"What kind of trouble?"

"I can't tell you just yet, but you could help him by going away for a few days. I remember he said you had a sister. You could go there. I'll take you. Trust me."

She'd been a fool, of course, but he must have known Leroy in order to know about her sister. She'd fallen into his trap. "How will my going away help Leroy?"

"The police may come around asking questions. It'd be better if you weren't here." He took her by the elbow and propelled her toward the door. "Get your coat and let's go."

Without thinking, she reached for her coat and started to follow him out. "Wait. I've got to call Leroy. Tell him where I'm going."

"There's no time." He grabbed a grocery list on the table, turned it over, groped in his pocket and brought out a pencil. He shoved them in front of her. "Here. Write him a note."

She'd quickly scrawled *Gone to Faye's*. They were out the door before she remembered her medications. "My medicine. I need my heart pills."

His hand tightened around her arm. "Not now. I'll come back for them when the coast is clear."

Malvina searched the street, expecting to see police cars converging around them. There was no one in sight. She hurried along to Joe's car, willing to go anywhere and do anything to help Leroy out of trouble.

"Faye lives in Lawton. We usually take Bogan Road north. It's shorter than the highway."

Joe just grunted. "Can make better time on the interstate."

It hadn't been until he turned off the interstate and had picked up a blacktop heading west that she'd become concerned. "This isn't the way to Lawton! Where are you taking me?" She grabbed at his right arm. "Take me back home. Take me to Leroy. Tell me what this is all about." He pulled his arm free, swung out, and backhanded her across the cheek. The blow hurled her head against the door frame, momentarily stunning her. She gasped for breath, clutched her chest as pain began to build, and whimpered like a lost puppy.

Malvina huddled in the seat as far from her abductor as possible, and dared not ask any more questions. She kept her eyes fixed on the roadside, noting every sign, every marker which she might need later either to find her way home or to describe to the police. She wondered why Joe hadn't bothered to blindfold her. Then came the frightening thought that he knew it wasn't necessary. He didn't intend her to travel that route ever again. But still she kept recording it in her mind. He turned off the blacktop to a winding gravel road with no signs and no houses. Behind the trees lining the road, she caught glimpses of water and knew they were following the Valley River. The river was running downstream toward Holliston, and they were driving upstream leaving home farther and farther behind. The wind had picked up. Proud trees bowed before its relentless force, funereal clouds obscured the sun, and Malvina's last little glimmer of hope flickered out.

They pulled up in front of a tiny rustic log cabin in a clearing surrounded by tall longleaf pines, red cedars, and bare water oaks. Joe walked around the car, opened the door, and motioned her out. Malvina wasn't sure her legs or her heart could obey. The sharp pain in her chest had subsided to a dull ache, but her limbs were as trembly as the naked branches above her. Malvina glared at the man in front of her, wondered if he would offer to help her, or if he would just yank her out of the car. It was something in-between. He took her right arm, pulled her toward him, steadied her as her feet wobbled to the ground. Without saying a word, he quickly escorted her to the cabin. He dropped her arm as he flipped his key-ring around, searching for the right one. There was no danger of her running away. He knew it, and she knew it.

She shivered as the frigid wind tore at her coat. Inside, it wasn't much warmer. "Sit down," Joe growled. "The john's that way," he added, pointing to a door in the rear of the room. Malvina didn't think her legs would hold her up long enough to make it to the bathroom, so she headed for the nearest chair. Joe kneeled before a dirt-brown kerosene heater that hugged the wall to her left. He turned a valve at its base, and she heard a whoosh as the heater quickened and began to breathe heat into the room.

Malvina assumed this was a hunting and fishing cabin meant to be occupied only by men. It consisted of one room plus what Joe called "the john." In the center of the room stood a square butcher-block table, suitable for cleaning fish, dining on squirrel, and playing poker.

Three or four times a year Leroy would take off for a weekend break with some guys. He never told her much about it, but at times he would brag about how many rabbits or squirrels he'd shot, or how much money he'd won. He never mentioned any losses. One time he had his picture taken with a deer he'd killed. She was sure this was the same cabin that was in the picture. When she asked why they never invited wives to go along, he'd answered, "You women wouldn't like it. It's just one room, cots stretched out along the walls, no TV. Nothing for women to do." So this was where Leroy had spent those weekends, and Joe was one of his buddies. Malvina's eyes teared up again. Did Leroy know that his friend had kidnapped her? Would her husband look for her? If so, would he find her in time?

While the room warmed, Joe opened cans in the kitchen area. Malvina decided her legs had recovered enough to make it to the bathroom. She had to check out any possible escape routes. What she found was a room barely big enough to turn around in, a commode with a broken seat, a sink featuring ice water, a one-walled shower stall, and a tiny window with a cracked pane.

After she came out, she hovered over the heater until

Joe slapped two bowls on the table. "Breakfast or lunch or whatever you want to call it." He had removed his coat but kept his cap in place. Without waiting for her, he began slurping the contents of his bowl. Malvina wasn't hungry, but knew she had to eat before she keeled over. The tomato soup was good even though it was mixed with water instead of with milk as she usually made it.

Joe finished his soup, propped his elbows on the table and stared at her. Malvina kept her eyes down to avoid his. He's trying to decide what to do next, she thought. She realized her kidnapping hadn't been planned. He'd done it on the spur of the moment because he was afraid she would call the police. If only she hadn't called out to him, she fussed at herself. She should have let him break into Allison's house and then called the cops. A tear escaped and splashed into her soup. She wiped at her eyes angrily. She had to think of a way out, she thought, instead of sitting here blubbering.

Joe stretched himself out of his chair, went over to a corner stashed with fishing gear, bent down and came up with a long piece of rope. "I've got to go. I'll just tie you up to keep you out of trouble while I'm gone."

The ritual had been repeated whenever he went out. When he was there, she was free to walk around the room, to look at old hunting magazines, even fix her own meals with whatever canned goods were in the kitchen. When he left, he tied her feet and her arms. She could lie down or sit up, even hop a little. Most of the time she tried to sleep. He was never gone more than four or five hours at a time and usually came back with food. Joe spoke little, refused to answer questions, often told her to shut up. When she'd begged him to get her heart medicines, he'd ignored her. She could tell he was worried. He kept looking out the window and always parked his car behind the cabin, so it couldn't be seen from the road.

Friday afternoon when he came back, she noticed a bulge under his jacket, just big enough for a gun. She had no doubt he intended to use it. She was actually relieved when he tied her up again, since that meant he was leaving. He came back late and left again early Saturday morning.

When he came back that afternoon, Malvina could tell he was even more agitated than usual. He'd stomped around the cabin, muttering to himself, glaring at her with eyes dark with hatred. He stayed just long enough to get her something to eat and left again. She'd been asleep when he slammed back in. He snapped on the light, jerked off his gloves and yanked the ropes as he untied them. His face was the picture of fury. For a moment she thought he was going to hit her. Instead he threw his jacket on the floor, snatched a beer from the refrigerator and started cussing.

His mood had improved by the time he had started out again Saturday evening. He seemed like a man with a plan.

Now it was Sunday afternoon, and she knew her time was running out. Her pulse was weak and thready without her Lanoxin. If Joe didn't kill her, her tired heart soon would. She wondered for the millionth time where Leroy was and if he was worried about her. She hoped Allison was all right. None of this was her fault. Allison had been a good, kind neighbor and now she might be in danger.

Malvina tried to ignore the pain as it grew into a crescendo, across her chest, down her left arm, up into her shoulder blade.

Her last conscious thought was to wonder how Joe would dispose of her body.

ELEVEN

ALLISON FELT AS IF she were on the witness stand that Sunday afternoon. After they finished eating, Fred made her repeat everything that had happened in the last week, then he fired questions to fill in any holes. Steve dispatched Gil and Tim to look in the yard again for any clue that might have been missed, while he and Martha sat and listened. Allison was uncomfortable with the role Fred was taking, and studied Steve's reaction. Steve seemed to be enjoying the scene. He'd heard it all before, but had his notebook out and jotted down an occasional note.

"Now tell me again just why you visited Malvina on Monday," Fred said.

"She had called and said she had something to give me."

"And what was that?"

"Last year's calendar."

Fred leaned back in his chair, ran his hand through thinning hair and gave her a puzzled look. "Why on earth would you want last year's calendar?"

Allison gave him a half-smile. Fred wasn't what anyone would call handsome, she thought, but he had a kind face with slightly chubby cheeks that made it hard for him to look serious. To compensate he could lower his voice to a frosty level when necessary. He did that now as he repeated his question. "So, why an old calendar?"

"Because teachers are born scavengers, that's why. We have to be. You know, with school budgets like they are." Fred shook his head, still not comprehending. Allison went on. "Schools don't give teachers money to buy extra classroom supplies, so I scrounge everything I can: old magazines, old calendars, even empty jars and toilet tissue rolls. It's amazing what kids can make with junk and imagination. And so I wanted the calendar pictures for the students to use on posters."

"I see." Fred grinned. "So school nowadays, isn't just readin' and writin', but playing with pretty pictures and making toilet paper people?"

Allison glared at him. "We in the profession feel it's teaching by letting students stretch their ingenuity and creativity. Besides," she went on, trying to suppress a smile, "it keeps their attention while I'm expounding on rather boring good health habits."

"Okay, I understand. But where is it now?"

"Where's what?"

"The calendar. There might be something on it that'll give an idea about where Malvina is. Her appointments. Her meetings."

"But how could knowing her appointments for last year help us now?"

Steve answered her question. "Because people tend to live in patterns. She may have had standing appointments or met with certain people on certain days. We might find some clue there."

"So-o-o," Fred drew the word out impatiently. "Where is this mysterious calendar?"

Allison's head went from side to side like an oscillating fan. Her brow furrowed. "I don't know," she finally said. "I don't really know where it is now. I intended to take it to school, but then forgot it."

Allison slapped the palm of her hand against her forehead. "How could I have been so dense? Of course, that must be it. The school break-in and then here. He, whoever he is, was looking for that calendar."

"That could be," Steve said. "I don't know why it didn't occur to us before."

"But what did I do with it?" Allison wandered into the den, stared at the piles of papers and magazines scattered around. Apparently Steve and the other officers had restored as much order as they could to the room after they finished their investigation, but there remained a lot to do. She shook her head. "When you people leave, I'll have to straighten out all this mess."

"Don't worry about that." Fred said. "I'll help you with it later. Right now we want to find the calendar. Of course, the culprit may have been successful in his search this time and the calendar is long gone."

Allison considered that possibility and shook her head. "I know I didn't put it in the basement. I seldom go down there. And if he had found the calendar up here, he would have had no reason to go downstairs."

Martha slid down to the floor by the magazines. "I'll look through these." She glanced up as Tim and Gil came into the room.

"Nothing out there," Tim reported.

Martha pointed to a pile of papers on the floor. "You boys want to tackle some of those."

"Yes Ma'am." Gil gave Martha a mock salute. He plopped down, leaned back against the side of the desk, stretched out his long legs, and grabbed a fistful of manila folders. "Now, teacher, tell me exactly what we're looking for."

"A calendar from last year," Allison answered.

"I'm sure even you know what a calendar looks like," Martha said. "It's one of those things that helps you count past ten and tells you when the Easter bunny is coming."

Allison's school teacher persona was fed up with the juvenile bickering between the two officers. She picked up a sofa pillow and pitched between them. "That's enough, you two. Cut the sarcasm and get busy." She was rewarded by two rueful smiles and two heads that bent down to their tasks. Steve glanced at her in surprise but didn't comment. Fred raised his eyebrows and nodded approvingly.

Allison dropped on the couch and contemplated the coffee table. "Now let me think. That's where it was the last time I saw it." Fred and Steve followed her gaze to the bare coffee table. "I remember now," she said. "It was slid halfway under the newspaper. I picked it up and looked at the beach scene. It reminded me of how much I love being by the ocean." Allison paused, her mind again picturing waves and sand.

Fred prompted her. "And then…?"

Allison jerked herself back to the present. "And then I tossed it back on the table. That's all I know."

"That can't be all," Fred insisted. "You did something else with it. It has to be in this house. What did you do next?" Fred's voice dropped several decibels, and Allison's face flushed with annoyance.

"Well, that's all I can remember. If it's still here, why don't *you* find it?" Allison immediately regretted her burst of ill temper. Fred was only here to help, and she really appreciated him driving so far to be with her today. She gave him an imploring look and mouthed, *Sorry.* He nodded in response.

Steve slipped down on the couch next to Allison and flipped his notebook. "Maybe we'd better put that on hold while we backtrack a little. Let me be sure I have this straight. Malvina gave you the calendar on Monday afternoon?"

Allison nodded. "And I saw it last on Wednesday night after I had tried to return Malvina's call, and Leroy told me she was already in bed. I remember that because I was too exhausted to read or do anything else. I looked briefly at the calendar and then went straight to bed."

"But you're sure you haven't seen it since then?" Fred asked, his voice now calm, an apologetic smile playing on his lips.

"I'm sure. Thursday after school I read most of the evening and of course Friday evening was spent looking for Malvina. I didn't notice the calendar. It was probably still on the coffee table. Yesterday morning I cleaned house like I always do and… That's it!" Allison bounced from the couch, climbed over Steve's outstretched legs and skidded into the kitchen. "The newspaper," she cried. The men hurried after her as she flung open the broom closet door, knelt down before a bright green recycling box and started tossing out old newspapers. Then with a grin which would do a Cheshire cat proud, she held aloft the missing calendar.

Both men reached out to grab it, but Steve, with his "detective in charge" voice, said, "I'll take that."

Fred quickly stepped back. "Be my guest." He laughed. Allison nodded her approval. Fred knew full well he was the guest here and that Steve could boot him out anytime.

They all returned to the kitchen. Steve sent Martha, Gil and Tim back out to finish canvassing the neighbors. Gil grabbed the last biscuit and munched happily on his way out.

Steve dropped the calendar on the kitchen table, pulled up a chair and turned the pages to January. "Now let's see what we have here."

Fred and Allison sat on either side of Steve and

hitched their chairs as close as possible to him. Steve ignored the pretty pictures which had intrigued Allison and studied the dates below. "January 12," he read, "Dr. L. 11:00."

"That's Dr. Larkin," Allison interpreted, "Malvina's cardiologist. She goes every month."

Steve gave a slight nod. "26th was Dr. D. 2:30."

"Must be Dr. Darnella, the dentist," Allison said. "I go to him too."

"Allison, you said Malvina didn't drive," Fred interrupted. "How did she get to her appointments?"

"Her sister often came down and drove her. Then they'd do lunch. If Faye couldn't come, Malvina would call Senior Services. They have a van that takes disabled and elderly people to various appointments and activities."

"Oh, yeah," Fred said. "I think our town has that service too. I just never paid much attention to it."

February's only notation was again Dr. L. except for a red circle around the 14th. "Wonder what that means?" Steve asked.

"It's obvious you don't have a steady girl, Steve," Allison said. "That's Malvina's reminder to Leroy to buy her Valentine candy or flowers. Some men have to be prompted, you know." Allison didn't dare look at Fred, but hoped he was making a mental note.

Steve turned to March. The week after Dr. L. was a note in a different handwriting. It read, *F-M 20/500* followed by a check mark. "Now what could that mean?" Allison asked.

"We'll figure it out," Steve said and shoved the calendar toward Fred. "You turn and I'll write." Steve copied down the date and the cryptic message while Fred turned to April. The same note was repeated in April on the Thursday before Easter. "I'm assuming," Steve said, "that these are Leroy's notes. I'll confirm it with him when he returns home."

"*If* he returns home," Fred said darkly.

The next month had two of the mysterious notes. The one on May 11th read, *C-V 100/100* and another one on May 23rd read *F-M 20/500*. Both were followed by check marks. Steve scribbled as Fred quickly turned the page. June had three entries: *F-M 20/1000, C-V 100/500 and again F-M 100/500.*

The rest of the year showed similar notes, using the same letters and numbers that occurred from ten days to two weeks apart. Steve copied them all down. "I'll have these typed up and study them later. Right now they don't make a bit of sense to me."

Allison took the calendar from Fred and studied it more closely. "One thing we do know is that the check marks weren't made at the same time as the entries."

Steve gave Allison a puzzled look. "And how do we know that?"

"Here, for instance," said Allison, pointing to an August entry. "The letters and numbers are in blue ink, but the check is in black ink." She flipped the page. "And here the check is in pencil."

"She's right, you know," Fred said, leaning over the

table in front of Steve. He patted Allison on the hand. "Good work, Partner." Allison gave a slight bow of her head, acknowledging the praise.

Steve took the calendar back and flipped through the rest of the pages. "Sure enough. It's obvious the checks were made at a later time. So what does that tell us?" He looked to either side of him. Allison shrugged, but Fred took the bait.

"It tells us that the notations indicate something Leroy had to do and when he had completed the task, he went back and checked it off." Fred stared at the December page where Steve had left it open. "Except here's one that didn't get checked off." Fred's finger slid by the 25th, circled in red, to the 28th. The entry read, *C-V 100/500* with no check mark behind it.

"Maybe that's why Leroy needed the calendar back," Allison suggested, "so he could check off his last assignment."

Fred frowned. "It's more likely he wanted it back because it was incriminating evidence. I don't know Leroy, never met him, but I'll bet my bottom dollar he was involved in some illegal trafficking. He was taking orders for something and checking it off when he delivered it."

"I agree," Steve said. "Now all we have to figure out is what and to who."

"To whom," Allison corrected him without thinking. Both men smiled, but Allison was too deep in thought to notice. "If Leroy was doing something illegal, why keep his records in such a public place? He could have hidden a notebook with this info very easily."

Steve answered. "From my interview with him Friday night, I came to a couple of conclusions. One—Leroy is not the sharpest tool in the shed. Two—he's been put down all his life, and he needed to feel important—if only to himself. Maybe just seeing the notations on the calendar every day fed his ego, made him feel like more than a simple maintenance man. He was probably very proud of the code he'd devised, knowing Malvina certainly wouldn't be able to decipher it. It may not have crossed his mind that anyone else would look at the calendar."

"But," Fred said, "Malvina must have been curious, asked him what the notations meant, or what they were for."

Allison nodded. "Sure she was curious. And knowing Malvina, she wouldn't have stopped asking. So Leroy must have come up with some simple explanation, and then told her it wasn't important."

"And she must have believed him," Steve added, "or she wouldn't have given the calendar away. But it was important to Leroy. He may have been worried that someone else seeing his coded entries would figure them out. He had to get the calendar back. Malvina, no doubt, told him that Allison wanted it for a school project. So he broke into the school to get it."

"It couldn't have been Leroy," Allison said. "He wouldn't have had time. Remember he left the house as usual, at six-thirty Wednesday morning. I heard him honk good-bye. The break-in must have been earlier than that to allow the intruder to finish before daybreak."

"And," Fred added, turning to Allison, "you told me Leroy and Malvina had only lived here for five years and had no children. When would he have been to your school? How would he have known which classroom was yours?" Fred drummed his fingers on the table, his right foot keeping time as if forcing his thoughts to march in step. It must have worked because he stopped his drumming, snapped his fingers and announced, "So he has a partner. His partner does know the school, knows your room, knows where you keep your supplies, or he finds out in some way. It should be an easy heist, but he strikes out because the calendar's not there. He tells Leroy. Now our friend has a real problem." Steve listened intently, nodding from time to time. "Leroy probably tells Malvina she must get the calendar back from Allison. That would account for her call to Allison Wednesday afternoon. Remember she said, 'It's important.'"

"But then why didn't Leroy let me talk to Malvina when I called back that night? And why did he make up that story about her going to Faye's?" Allison looked at Fred as if he should know all the answers.

Fred took a deep breath and let it out slowly. "Don't know. We actually don't know anything. We need some facts instead of conjectures."

"Well, there is one fact we know," Allison said.

The two men gave her their complete attention. "And what's that?" Steve asked.

Allison was enjoying her moment in the limelight and intended to prolong it as long as she could. She stretched. She ran her fingers through her short hair. She poured herself another glass of tea and finally said, "We know the letters are not a person's first and last initials."

"Okay, I give up," Steve said. "Explain, please."

"Remember I'm a teacher. I notice these things."

"For heaven's sake. What things?" Fred burst out.

Allison laughed and relented. "A person's initials are written as F period M period, or simply as FM with no punctuation. You don't put a dash or a hyphen between the first and last initial."

"Yeah, I guess you're right," Steve said. "So maybe it's the initials of a company that hyphenates its name. Like Scott-Harrelson Tire Company."

"It could be," Fred said without enthusiasm.

"Well," the young detective said to the older one, "do you have any ideas?"

Fred shook his head.

"He has to let it simmer," Allison said. Steve gave her a questioning look. "You see," she explained, "Fred told me detective work is like making a gourmet pot of beef stew. You have to let it simmer. You can't try to bring it to a boil too soon." Steve looked at Fred, but Fred had taken a sudden interest in yellow daisies on the kitchen wallpaper.

"Well," Steve said, trying to keep the amusement out of his voice, "I guess we all have our different approaches. I'm a fast food man myself." He ran his hand over his mouth. "Now let's go back to your previous question, Mrs. A., about why Leroy wouldn't let you talk to Malvina Wednesday night."

"All right. Why?"

"Because he'd changed his mind, or he decided he'd get the calendar back by himself, or she had already gone missing."

"That may be it," Fred said. "Malvina became a threat to his operation, whatever that was, and he had to get rid of her." Fred turned to Steve. "You did use Luminal on the house, didn't you?"

It was Steve's turn to study the daisies. "No," he answered slowly. "At the time it didn't seem indicated. There were no signs of a struggle."

Allison recalled reading about Luminal in one of her recent murder mysteries. She knew it could detect blood on a surface even though it had been scrubbed clean. Reading about it, though, was a lot easier than thinking it might be needed at a neighbor's house. "Surely you don't think Leroy would actually harm Malvina. Do you?" Allison shook her head. "I know Leroy. He loves his wife. He takes care of her. He treats her like a fragile doll."

"Apparently neither you nor Malvina knew Leroy as well as you thought you did," Fred said, giving Allison a sad smile. "It happens."

She didn't want to dwell on that thought any longer.

"What about last night? It certainly wasn't Leroy I saw in the ski mask. It was someone taller, thinner, younger."

"How do you know he was younger if you couldn't see his face?" Steve asked.

Allison thought. "Just an impression, I guess." She got up, walked to the hallway and faced the basement door, trying to reenact the scene in her mind. "It was the way he held the bat," she said. "That's it. He held the bat away from his chest, upward, in batting position." Allison knew a correct batting stance. "He held it like a bat, not like a club. It was probably instinctive." Allison's voice held no doubt. "He was a young man who plays baseball."

"The partner again," Fred muttered.

Steve broke in before Fred could say anything else, "We'll get right on it, find out who Leroy's associates were—work, play, church, clubs."

"It won't be a long list," Allison said. "The only place Leroy ever went was to work and hunting and fishing."

"Well, wherever he's at this weekend," Fred said, "I doubt the fish are biting."

Steve started wrapping things up for the day. Martha, Tim and Gil reported in. No one had seen a strange car or a ski-masked man the previous night. "Not that I'm surprised," Gil said. "They were either watching the Bull's game or the re-re-rerun of Star Wars."

The repair men from *Windows, Etc.* had finished installing a new glass patio door. This one was shatter-proof. Allison was anxious to start restoring order to her house.

Fred hunched over the calendar, still trying to translate Leroy's notes, until Steve reached for it and Fred handed it over. "How about running me off a copy of each month, Steve? That is, if you don't mind an old man playing with your toys."

"Fine," Steve said. "I'll take this by the office and send the copies back. Want me to copy the pretty pictures for you too?"

Martha brought back the calendar copies later that afternoon. Steve had sent a set for each of them with a note. *Happy simmering!* Allison giggled. Fred didn't.

Allison dragged out the vacuum cleaner and went over the entire house, trying to eradicate every trace of the man who had trespassed into her private life. She pulled out couches and ferreted under beds. She swept around chairs, under tables and behind doors. When she finally flipped the off-switch, Fred gave a sigh of relief.

"Satisfied now?"

Allison grinned. "I guess it'll do until I can get an exorcist in here."

Fred took the length of the room in two long strides, put his arms around her, drew her head to his shoulder, whispered into her ear, "I can spend the night if you want me to."

TWELVE

SEVERAL SECONDS PASSED before Allison raised her head and kissed him lightly on the lips. She wasn't sure what his offer meant, but he had to be more explicit than that before she jumped into his arms. "Thanks, but you need to get back to work, and I need to learn to be alone again. I'll be all right."

"Sure you will." Fred stepped back, brushed some hair out of Allison's eyes. "But I'm not so sure I will." He hesitated. "Worrying about you, I mean."

"The best cure for worry is work, and that's what both of us are going to do tomorrow. Right now, I have a special job for you. Then I'm going to take you out to dinner and send you on your way."

"But I have to work for my dinner?"

"That's right. I bought a painting at the art show last night and it needs to be hung right above my desk." Allison went to the hall closet and brought out the painting. She propped it against the recliner, tilted her head and studied her purchase. She turned to Fred. "Well, what do you think?"

Fred rubbed the back of his neck, scrunched up his

lips. "If I said it looked like a monkey painting would you be mad at me forever?"

Allison glared at him and then returned her gaze to the painting. It was the first time she had actually studied it. The base of the picture consisted of scrambled triangles and rectangles in shades of dull brown and gray mixed with jet-black circles and one wine-red square. The center of the painting was the yellow of spring dandelions. The yellow rippled across the canvas, getting brighter and brighter. Toward the top of the painting luminous shafts of oranges and reds joined with the yellows until the colors seemed to explode out of the frame. Allison giggled. "You mean a monkey gone wild in a paint factory?"

"Something like that." Fred leaned closer and read the title out loud. "Breakthrough." He stepped back and nodded his head. "You know, in a strange kind of way, it does say something."

"You think?"

"Yeah. You see that mess at the bottom, the dark colors, maybe that's our mundane lifestyle. Maybe we've missed a lot of sunlight in our lives. But it doesn't have to stay that way. We can come up to the light and break out of our humdrum existence. Make a breakthrough and live life to its fullest."

Allison gaped at Fred, her mouth hanging half opened. "Wow. A side of you I haven't seen before. Where did Mr. Art Connoisseur come from?"

Fred shook his head and Allison thought it looked

like he was blushing. "Don't pay any attention to me. Just got carried away there for a minute. Where do you want this lovely work of art?"

Allison pointed to the spot above her desk. "Then I can lounge on the couch and contemplate living life to the fullest." She headed toward the kitchen. "I'll get the toolbox."

It took only ten minutes and one hit thumb to hang the painting. Allison stood back and admired it. Fred took her by the shoulders and pointed her toward the door. "Let's find that dinner you promised me. It's been a long time since lunch."

THEY WENT OUT TO EAT at The Lighthouse. The restaurant used to be referred to as a fish camp, but new owners had upscaled their image with a sign reading *Seafood and Steaks,* added tablecloths, lowered the lights, and upped the prices. The result was fewer Harleys and more tourists. That was fine with Allison. She was glad there was at least one fine dining place in her little town she could show off to Fred.

The waiter lit the candle at their table and took their order. Fred went for the rib-eye, medium rare, while Allison opted for flounder. But their minds were not on food. "Now until they catch this guy, you've got to promise me to be extra careful," Fred said. "No late-night meetings, no letting strangers in, no snooping around. And when Leroy comes home, you are not to make any neighborly visits. Understand?"

Allison smiled and nodded. It was nice to have someone concerned about her besides her kids. Connie and Dave had both called that afternoon, their usual Sunday ritual, but she hadn't told them about the break-ins, or about Malvina being missing. They already had too much on their minds with all their studying for her to add to it. She'd just mentioned that Fred had come up for a visit, knowing they would be pleased.

He spoke briefly to each of them, told them to study hard, to stay out of trouble, and not to worry about their mother. She gave him a peck on the cheek for it.

Now, in the restaurant, she relaxed and reveled in Fred's solicitude. "I promise I'll behave," she said.

"And call me every night?"

"Well, maybe not every night," she demurred.

"Then I'll call you."

"Fine."

Fred sipped his coffee and smiled at her. "Now let's change the subject and talk about something nice."

"And that would be?"

"For instance, have you been writing any poetry lately?"

Allison couldn't have been happier with his choice of topics. It was in a restaurant like this last summer when she'd first shared with him her love of poetry and her attempts at writing it. He'd been a marvelous listener and later on had even written a poem for her.

She nodded her head. "As a matter of fact I wrote one about spring in the motel last night."

"Spring? Aren't you getting a little ahead of the seasons?"

"I had to do something to get my mind off the terrible things that have been happening. So I projected forward to spring. Then my mind jumped back several decades and I remembered spring when I was growing up—when my little world was safe and everything was new and beautiful."

"Sounds like a marvelous poem. Let's hear it."

"It's free verse so don't expect rhyme or rhythm. It goes like this:

Spring prances through town
wearing azaleas and peach blossoms.
Her lips pucker at the tangy taste
of wild strawberries.
She tosses out the first ball and
the sound of a cracking bat
is heard in the land.
Then she joins squealing children
squishing mud through bare toes.

Allison threw up her hands. "So. Do you think Robert Frost would approve?"

"Definitely. It brings back memories of my childhood except that my mother would never let me play barefoot in the mud."

"Then you have missed one of the all-time joys of life. Maybe later on I can teach you the fine art of squishing mud."

"It's a date. And I'm glad you were able to escape from reality, for a while at least."

Allison crunched a crisp hush puppy and toyed with her slaw. Then she raised her head, and a tear slid down her cheek. "But my escape didn't last long. I got to thinking about poor Malvina, and I just know something terrible has happened to her, and I vowed that whoever is responsible will pay dearly. Then I scribbled a parody to vent my fury."

"A parody. Is that when you take off on something previously written? Aren't they usually funny?"

"They can be, but this isn't. Remember the folk song, *Down In The Valley?*"

Fred nodded and sang softly.

"Down in the valley,
The valley so low.
Hang your head over,
Hear the wind blow."

"Right," Allison said, "and then there's a verse that goes,

Write me a letter.
Send it by mail.
Send it in care of
The Birmingham jail.

"So this is how I changed it.

Down in our valley,
Our valley forlorn
Hang your head over,
Hear the wind moan.
I'll write you a letter.
I'll send it by mail.
Cause you're never leaving
That cold, cold jail."

Fred reached for her hand. "Terrible poetry but the right sentiment. Don't worry, the culprits will be caught and sent away and never bother your peaceful valley again." His fingers curled around hers. "But in the meantime, you leave it to the police."

ALLISON HAD MEANT IT when she promised Fred she would do no detecting and no snooping. But that was before Steve called the next day to tell her they'd found Leroy's body.

THIRTEEN

ALLISON SHOVED THE weekend's events to the back of her mind, and tried to pretend this was a typical Monday morning at Madison Middle School. This illusion was shattered when Mr. Forster's secretary called her to the office for a phone call. She flinched as Steve gave her the news.

"A mill worker found Leroy's body when he went in this morning. Crushed to death in one of the machines." Steve paused and Allison heard him take a deep breath. "It was a machine used to pick up and move large rolls of cloth. I don't know how he got caught in it, but it crushed his upper body and left him dangling upside down."

"Oh, no." Allison felt a cold shiver go through her. "But Leroy had worked on those machines for years. How could an accident like that have happened?"

"Maybe it *wasn't* an accident."

Allison clutched the phone tighter in her hand. "You don't think so?"

"I don't know. Everyone else seems to think so. Mr. Crandall says the machine was reported to be acting up Friday afternoon and he'd asked Leroy to look at it. But before Leroy had a chance to check it out, he was called home."

"That was when I called him," Allison interrupted, "about Malvina."

"Yes," Steve said. "And then we took him down to the police station, so he didn't get back to work that day. Crandall thinks he must have come in on Saturday or Sunday to fix it and somehow got caught. Since he was alone in the plant, no one heard his cries for help."

"How horrible." Allison shuddered again as she imagined Leroy being trapped by the monster machine and his unheard screams. But her mind rebelled against the even more ghastly thought that it may not have been an accident. "You know, he might have been so upset about Malvina, he got careless."

"Maybe," Steve said, "but if he was so worried about his wife, why wasn't he out looking for her? Why go to the mill? I doubt the machine had to be repaired immediately."

Allison pondered this while Mr. Forster glared at her. "I've got to get back to my class, Steve," she said. "Call me tonight, or better yet, come by the house and catch me up on everything. I'll make a fresh pot of coffee."

She turned to Mr. Forster as she hung up the phone. "Did Steve tell you what happened?"

"Yes. But I don't see how an accident at Valley Mill affects you."

"Anything that affects my neighbors affects me,"

she snapped back. "I agree with Donne that *No man is an island.*"

She was already riled with him. Mr. Forster didn't seem to be interested in anything except what happened at the school.

Earlier that morning Allison had tried to update him on the weekend's happenings. His only response had been, "Your intruder was probably just a copycat. I hope Steve isn't going to let that little distraction deter him from working on *our* case."

Little distraction? Allison was indignant. If that's his attitude, she thought, I won't say another word about the matter.

Mr. Forster knew about Malvina being missing, of course. He'd been at the art show and must have heard the buzz about it. This morning Allison had had a wild notion to tease Mr. Forster about Lorraine and her seafoam cookies, but then decided she didn't dare. No one teased Mr. Forster. It was just as well. Now she was angry with him. He didn't consider the break-in at her house or Malvina's disappearance of any importance, and apparently, not even the gruesome death of Malvina's husband.

As soon as she arrived home that afternoon, Allison called Fred at his office. He wasn't in. "No. No message," she said, "I'll catch him later." It'd been a long day. At lunch time she'd flipped on the radio in the teacher's lounge to catch the midday news. They reported an unfortunate industrial accident in Holliston. A local man was crushed to death in a textile machine. His name was being withheld pending notification of his next of kin. Allison wondered about his next of kin. In her heart, she felt Malvina no longer qualified for that position.

Allison was finishing her soup and salad when Steve and Martha drove up. They greeted each other like friends at a funeral—glad to see each other, but wishing it was under happier circumstances. Allison shooed them into the den and soon followed with chocolate grahams and coffee. Martha curled up on the couch, Steve chose the recliner, and Allison dropped into the rocker. Steve made church steeples with his fingers and studied the ceiling. "I guess it could have been an accident," he said. "Crandall insists that it was. But it's hard to figure out how Leroy got caught in the machinery."

Allison waited for him to go on, but Steve unwrapped another piece of gum to join the one already in his mouth. The silence became too long. Allison recalled the first question her favorite fictional detectives usually posed, so she asked, "How long had he been dead?"

"About twenty-four hours. Maybe longer." Steve took a determined breath, chewed several times and went on. "The cause of death was massive trauma to his head and chest. But it was definitely Leroy. His face was still identifiable. I asked the ME to do a dental check anyway, though, so there couldn't be any question."

Allison was worried about Steve. He looked exhausted; he needed a shave; his eyes brooded. She wished she could go to him, pat him on the back, say something comforting, but she knew that was not what he needed or wanted. He needed some assurance that he could handle this case, both emotionally and professionally. And she knew he would have to find that surety in his own way, in his own time. Allison looked away and left him to his thoughts.

She turned to Martha. "What do you think?"

Martha reached for another cracker and sipped her coffee. "I didn't go to the mill. From what I've heard there are several unanswered questions. For instance, why was the machine running if Leroy was working on it? It doesn't make sense to try to repair a machine that's running."

"Maybe he turned it on to diagnose the problem before starting his repair," Allison suggested. "You know, the way the garage mechanic listens to your motor and then tells you the thingamabob needs a new whatchamacallit."

"I guess that could be it. And he got caught before he had a chance to turn it back off. Steve said his tools were out and he had grease on his hands."

Allison smiled. "Leroy always had grease on his hands. Malvina used to make him scrub with Ajax, but even that didn't get it all off." Allison's face sobered as she thought of poor Malvina. "Any news about her?"

Martha shook her head. "Steve sent Tim and me back over to the Hastings house this morning, after the report on Leroy." Martha stifled a yawn. "This was supposed to be my day off, but Gil called in sick, so I had to come in. I should never have watched that late movie last night."

Allison's detecting genes leaped into action. Gil. Gil had shown an unusual interest in her house when he accompanied her home Wednesday night. He didn't work on Thursday and Malvina hadn't been seen since Thursday. He called in sick today. What was he up to now? She wished she knew more about his background and about the antagonism that seemed to exist between him and Martha. But, she reasoned, now was not the right time to ask. Maybe she could get Martha alone at some point and find out more.

Martha's voice interrupted Allison's train of thought. "Anyway, we didn't find anything at the house we didn't already know. We used Luminal in several places just in case there was blood around. Again nothing. We asked her sister to come down and look it over, but she couldn't find anything out of place or unusual. She didn't think any clothes had been taken. Of course, with Malvina's medications and makeup still there, it's pretty obvious she left hurriedly and probably against her will."

"Do you think she'll ever be found?"

Martha shrugged. "Faye asked me the same thing. I tried to be optimistic with her—said we were following every lead, broadcasting her picture statewide, interviewing everybody we could think of." She looked at Steve, who was still staring into space, and then turned her attention back to Allison. "To tell the truth, I think we'll find her body. But we'll not get to the bottom of any of this until we solve the puzzle of the calendar."

Steve came alive and stretched out of his chair. "And the best way to do that is to find Leroy's partner. If Leroy's death was murder, then his phantom partner is the prime suspect." He headed for the door with Martha scrambling close behind. "How about calling your boyfriend, Mrs. Aldridge? Maybe he's simmered up some ideas."

As soon as her guests left, Allison did just that. Fred was quiet as she relayed the latest happenings. Then in an attempt to add a little humor, she said, "As my students like to say, 'Things are getting worser and worser.'"

But Fred was in no mood for levity. "It wasn't an accident," he said in a grim voice. "Someone needed to silence Leroy before he spilled his guts. Or, Leroy knew who had abducted his wife and was threatening him."

"His partner?" Allison had been thinking of this elusive character much of the day. She agreed with Steve, that if they could find him, they would find the answers. She had described him to herself several times: tall, thin, young, plays baseball, wears black, knew she'd be gone Saturday evening, and probably has an illegal source of money. She knew who fit nearly every bit of that description.

She hesitated, but she had to ask Fred to help. "Do you know anybody in the Charlotte police department?"

"Yeah, a couple of fellows. Went to college with one

and another officer I knew well moved to Charlotte a couple of years ago." Allison could almost hear his brain shifting into gear. "Why"

"Could they do a background check on Gil Watts? He's from Charlotte."

"What? That kid? I agree he can be obnoxious, but that's hardly enough reason to accuse him of murder."

"I'm not accusing him of anything. But I do have some doubts about him. Some things about him just don't add up."

"Such as?"

Allison could picture Fred right now, phone in his left hand, pencil in right, his brow furrowed deeper than a newly plowed field, his eyes full of questions. She had her answers ready. "Number one, he drives a new Eldorado that he could hardly afford on a cop's pay. Two, he arrived at school after the break-in looking like he'd donned his uniform in a hurry. Three, he was off duty Thursday and called in sick today. Also, he wasn't working the night of my break-in, but he arrived here a few minutes later. Four, he wears a lot of black. Five, he looks like a baseball player."

Allison could tell Fred was trying to keep his voice solemn. "Pretty damaging case. There ought to be a law against boys who wear black and play baseball."

"Okay, laugh if you want to, but I'm serious. Will you do it for me? I can't ask Steve to investigate someone in his own department. At least, not until I have something more than vague suspicions."

"Sure, I'll see what I can find out. In the meantime, you keep out of it. Don't tell anybody of your suspicions about Gil—or anyone else. There's a dangerous man loose in your lovely little town, and we know he doesn't mind killing people. In fact, there may be more than one dangerous person."

"What do you mean?"

"Leroy may have had more than one partner. We can't dismiss any possibilities."

FOURTEEN

THE NEXT MORNING Allison was tempted to call in sick. I could claim mental and emotional exhaustion, she thought. It was hard for her to believe it'd been less than a week since her life had jumped aboard this crazy roller coaster. Her mind skittered around like a scared rabbit while she was dressing. Murder, kidnapping, secret codes, good guys who could be bad guys; it was all too much. She reached into her closet and brought out the only red blouse she owned. She had to have at least one cheerful spot in her life today to make it through.

The school day crept by like a movie scene in slow motion. Her red blouse and the warm winter sunshine did little to lift her spirits. During gym class, she told the girls they could choose between shooting baskets and running around the track. They were out the door in a wink's time, eager to get out in the sun.

On her way home, Allison decided she couldn't avoid the supermarket any longer. With all the recent happenings, she'd neglected her weekly shopping trip. The few snacks she'd picked up Friday evening were gone.

There were several shoppers and only two cashiers. Little Miss Perky with her wide smile and pink hair bow had three loaded carts parked in her aisle. Allison reluctantly chose the other lane. She pushed her cart toward the cashier who could easily have played Disney's Grumpy. He was not new to Allison. They had often stared at each other over celery stalks, Rome apples, and baloney. He, with his basset hound chin and tired eyes; she, with an understanding smile. She'd tried polite conversation in the past and he'd only grunted. Today she was too tired to even try.

When the scanner finished its rhythmic beeping, he pointed to the total. It was $38.53. Allison fished in her billfold for a couple of twenties. She saw only a hundred and a five. She handed him the big bill and waited for change. To her surprise, his lips started moving. "Can't take that," he growled. His voice sounded rusty, like a saw that had been left out in the rain.

"For heaven's sake, why not?" She made no effort to hide her irritation. The sign by the register read, *No bills higher than twenty after eleven p.m.* It was now only four-thirty. "You can't be out of change already."

He shoved the bill in front of her. "It's no good," he said. Allison cringed as she saw an ugly black smear across Ben Franklin's face.

Some son of a gun, she realized, had stuck her with a counterfeit bill. Who? When? And was there any way to cut her loss? To a school teacher, a hundred dollars was a lot of money. Her thoughts went to Steve. He'd said the merchants weren't using the magic pen. She fumed under her breath. Who would have thought Old Grumpy would actually follow a police suggestion?

Allison reached out for the funny money, but Grumpy snatched it back and, at the same time, grabbed the mike by his register and barked out, "Mr. Perkins. Register five. Now!" Faces swerved, voices hushed, Allison wanted to slide under the counter.

The manager hurried up. He and Allison had a nodding acquaintance. He nodded now as he stroked the hundred-dollar bill. "Let's go back to my office," he said quietly.

"But what about my groceries?" Allison protested. "There's ice cream in there."

"This won't take long. I just have to call the police."

When Mr. Perkins hung up the phone in his office, he again nodded. "The officer said you could go on home. He'll send someone out later to question you." The manager stared at Allison a few moments before adding, "I'll let you write a check for the groceries since I know you."

Allison didn't waste any time. She wrote the check, handed it to Mr. Perkins, and fled.

She'd barely put away the groceries when a patrol car drove up. She held her breath until she saw Martha getting out. Thank goodness, it wasn't Gil. When Allison opened the door, Martha greeted her with a smile and a hug. It may not have been professional, but it was just what she needed.

"I hear you have a little extra-curricular activity going on." Martha tittered as she pulled out a chair and waved the counterfeit bill in the air. "I knew the governor should have pushed harder for a teacher pay raise."

"Very funny. And I thought you were my buddy. Just for that, I ought not to give you one of the chocolate eclairs I tried to pay for with tainted money."

"I'm sorry. No more smart remarks." Martha tried to look contrite. "But please don't deprive me of my chocolate high."

Allison placed two tantalizing goodies on the table along with coffee. No police business was discussed until the last crumb had disappeared and their lips were wiped free of chocolate. These ladies understood priorities.

"Now," Martha said, pulling out her notebook, "who conned you with the phony?"

"I wish I knew." Allison absently stirred her coffee. "But I do know it was at the art show. I remember Lorraine Rogers came up to me and asked if I had change for a hundred. The cashier was running low on small bills. I was pouring punch at the time, but no one was at the table, so I went to the cabinet and got my purse. She gave me the hundred and I handed her four twenties, a ten and two fives. I'm positive I didn't open my billfold again until this afternoon. I always give a check at church, and I hadn't bought anything."

"So Lorraine may know where it came from?"

"I doubt it. She was just trying to find change for

Buck Franklin. He's the treasurer of the Arts Council and was keeping the cash box. You really need to talk to him. He may remember who gave him big bills."

"Where would I find Buck? And is Buck a real name or is it short for Buckaroo?" Martha laughed at her own little joke as she scribbled in her notebook.

Allison gave her an appreciative grin. "His real name is Buford, but nobody calls him that except his mother. He's at Middleton Insurance. They're closed by now, but I have his home phone number."

"Before I call him," Martha said, "clear something up for me. I've never been to one of your art shows, but it seems to me that most people would use checks or charge cards for such major purchases. Or am I wrong?"

"Most of them do write checks, and we don't take credit cards. However, you must keep in mind that these are local artists. Many of the paintings and sketches are unframed, and the prices for some may be under fifty dollars. So people do often pay cash for those items."

"Explain how it works," Martha said. "Don't the artists collect the money themselves?"

"No. Each artist prices his own work, but the Art Council collects the money. A ticket on each item gives the artist's name and the price. After the show, the tickets are added up and the artists receive the amount of their sales, minus our commission. The Art Council uses the fees to pay for advertising and expenses."

"Okay, so I guess my next stop is with Buck."

Martha yawned and stretched. "I was supposed to be off an hour ago. These long hours are getting to me."

"You do look tired." Allison looked worriedly at the policewoman. "Gil out sick again?"

"No. He showed up. He and Steve spent most of the day at Valley Mill investigating Mr. Hastings' death. I haven't heard anything from them."

"Martha," Allison began, "it's really none of my business. And I probably shouldn't say anything, but…" Allison paused to decide how to ask what she wanted to ask.

Martha laughed. "But what? Go ahead. Ask."

"Well, it's nothing important. It's just that I've noticed you and Gil don't seem to get along very well. Any particular reason?"

Martha shrugged her slim shoulders. "Nothing in particular. He simply rubs me the wrong way. When he first joined the department, he tried the 'poor me' routine, telling us he'd been raised on the wrong side of the tracks and had pulled himself up by his own bootstraps. I had a hard time believing that. He has good manners, when he wants to use them, he's obviously well educated, and he always has plenty of money to spend. But the thing that really bugs me is that he seems to go out of his way to irritate people, especially me. He knows my marriage is in trouble, and he can't keep his mouth shut about it."

"Strange. It's an odd way to make friends."

"I know. He doesn't seem to want to get close to

anyone in the department. Who knows why? It's really a shame. Especially now when we all need to work together. We're just not staffed for the crime wave we're having."

Allison winced. "That certainly describes the situation. I feel like I've been slapped by a monster wave and can't hold my head above the water. Any news at all?"

"Not really. Leroy's brother from Virginia will claim his body when the medical examiner releases it. No final autopsy report yet." Martha rose to leave and tucked the counterfeit bill into her notebook. "And now we've got this to worry about. Actually, though, the Secret Service handles all counterfeit money cases."

"Secret Service? That seems strange. Why is it their jurisdiction?"

"Federal crime. And the Secret Service is a bureau of the Treasury Department. They protect not only our president but our currency, as well. All we'll be doing is a little leg work for them."

"I see," Allison said. "And nothing on Malvina? I'm going crazy thinking about her, worrying about her."

Martha shook her head. "You know Steve called in the SBI?"

"No, I didn't know. What prompted that?"

"I guess he thinks time might be running out for Mrs. Hastings in view of her medical condition, and he wants to do everything possible to find her."

Martha paused as she opened the door. "I don't want to alarm you, but do be careful. Remember, two people who knew about the calendar are already victims. I don't want anything to happen to you."

Martha's concern took Allison by surprise. When Fred had cautioned her, she'd tried to brush it off. Coming from Martha the warning seemed more sinister. Was she really in danger?

FIFTEEN

HER APPETITE FOR DINNER thoroughly spoiled, Allison picked up the *Holliston Journal*. The front page of the special edition screamed the news of the past week. Malvina and Leroy smiled out from their anniversary picture. Allison had often seen the photo sitting on their bookcase next to the TV. Malvina had pointed it out proudly the first time Allison had gone over to welcome the newcomers. In the ensuing five years the two women had become, not close friends, but caring neighbors.

The paper held no information she didn't already know, but seeing it in print banished any illusion that Holliston was still a safe little town. Separate stories dealt with the missing person, the industrial accident, the school break-in, and her own burglary. Each story ended with similar words, *The police are continuing their investigation.* Allison knew Steve and the SBI were doing their best, but she was beginning to wonder if that would be enough.

The review of the art show had been relegated to page four. Allison nodded in agreement as she read the polite, cautious comments. Holliston had no outstanding artists, but the exhibitors were praised for their *development*. The candid photos caught the essence of the show: artists trying to look nonchalant, browsers attempting deep study, students checking their watches. Allison gave each a moment's glance, then paused when she came to a picture of two men, standing at the back of the room, apparently in earnest conversation. She easily recognized her former student, Wally Stitson, and recalled their conversation that evening about his artistic talent. After closer examination, she determined his companion was Rufus Crandall. Her forehead frowned in puzzlement. How do those two know each other? And why, she wondered, would the owner of Valley Textile Mill be hobnobbing with a young kid like Wally? Allison made a mental note to find out what line of work Wally was in. Even if he worked at the mill, it wasn't likely he'd have social connections with the owner. Allison dropped the paper and rubbed her head. Stop trying to complicate things, she scolded herself. At public events, people always meander around and chat with each other. There are enough mysteries around here without trying to add more, she thought. Still, she wondered what they'd been talking about.

Allison decided Fred ought to be home by now and dialed his number. Just hearing his voice was enough to calm her nerves. He answered louder than necessary, "Hel-LO-O." His emphasis on the last syllable made Allison visualize the greeting accompanied by a big smile.

She squeaked out a thin, "Hi, how are you?"

"Great. And you?"

"Not so great, but tell me your story first."

"For starters, there was a touch of spring in the air today."

"Spring?" Allison hoped her voice conveyed the proper skepticism. "It's only the first week of February. You must be hallucinating, as I was when I wrote that poem."

"Hon, this is the South, and I'm further south than you are. Here, spring isn't dependent on the calendar. All it takes are some sunny days, a crazy peach tree pushing out an unseasonable blossom, and a mockingbird auditioning for an angel choir."

Allison didn't grasp all the ingredients of his spring. In fact, she'd stopped listening after the first word. It'd been a long while since she'd been "Hon" to anybody. It felt warm and cuddly and yes, like spring. She murmured a soft, "Um-m-m," unable to come up with any intelligent response.

Fred's voice shifted to his business mode. "I think you're on the wrong track with Gil. He checks out fine. Graduated from high school with decent grades, played most of the sports, no recorded trouble. He took a couple of courses in auto mechanics at the community college. His dad sold cars, mother worked in an office. They were killed in an accident last year and Gil moved away. He's got a sister in Raleigh, other scattered kinfolk. As far as I could find out, he's just a typical, middle-class kid, trying to make something of himself."

Fred paused. Allison didn't say anything. Fred asked hesitantly, "Doesn't that satisfy you?"

"Oh, sure. Thanks a lot for your trouble. I'm glad to hear that Gil's okay." Something nagged at the back of her mind, but she pushed it away. "I guess I was just being silly."

"So what else is new?" Fred caught his breath. "I didn't mean that the way it sounded. You definitely are not a silly person, Allison. But sometimes detectives can go sniffing up a wrong tree and lose the real trail." Allison laughed and Fred countered with a gruff, "What are you laughing at?"

"Us. I was picturing you and me as a couple of coon dogs, noses to the ground, drooling at the mouth, and ears flapping as we close in on our prey." Allison sighed. "If only we knew who we were after."

"Has Steve come up with anything yet?"

Allison filled Fred in on what little she knew of the investigation. Then when she could no longer put it off, she told him of her unfortunate encounter with the funny money. "And don't you dare laugh at me," she ended, "or I'll never speak to you again."

Fred's voice was serious. "It's no laughing matter. These counterfeiters are enlarging their area. Bills are showing up in several new places. We all have to be on our guard."

"Believe me, I'm going to be. Right now, though, I'm heading for bed and I'm going to put everything out of my mind."

"Sleep well," Fred said. "I'll call you tomorrow."

Allison took three aspirins, pulled her covers up to her chin, and tried to relax. It didn't happen. She got up and fixed a cup of decaf. On her way back to bed, she picked up her copy of the now infamous calendar pages. Lancelot joined her, nosed around for just the right spot, found it, turned around twice, tucked his front paws under his chin, and promptly dozed off. "Fat lot of company you are," Allison complained. "You could at least stay awake long enough to discuss Leroy's blasted cryptograms. Now I'll have to talk to myself." She took a sip of coffee and flipped through the months. "They start in March and end in December, so whatever it was, the venture lasted less than a year. Of course, it would probably still have been going on if I hadn't messed things up by asking for the calendar." Allison shook her head to exorcize the visions of the missing Malvina and the dead Leroy reeling in her mind. "I can't think of them now. I've got to concentrate on this."

She propped her pillow up higher behind her back and stared at Dave's picture on her dresser. He was grinning and holding a basketball to one side so his number 21 could be seen. The picture had been snapped the night he scored twenty-one points in a crucial game.

Allison forced her eyes away from the happy number to the puzzling ones in front of her. "All the numbers before the slash are 20 or 100," she muttered, "and the numbers after the slash are either100, 500, or 1000. But what are they? Leroy worked in the textile mill. Was he smuggling out bolts of cloth? Was it some kind of gambling scheme? And what about C-V and F-M?

"Are they people, companies, sports teams, products?" Allison dropped the paper on the floor and flipped off the lamp. "I give up. I guess you've got the right idea, Lancelot. I'll just have to sleep on it."

And she did. It was a fitful sleep filled with dreams of lottery numbers, masked kidnappers, Gil and Martha fussing, Malvina on a cruise ship looking calm and peaceful, Fred simmering a pot of stew, Dave running and twisting and squirming down the court, Gil hitting a home run, Leroy checking off his calendar entries. She watched them all from a distance, a cup of coffee in one hand and a coon dog's leash in the other. The dog was sniffing at each tree and bush without much interest, but when he came to Gil's red car, the dog lifted one leg and relieved himself on a tire. Gil didn't see the incident because he was waving at his mother. Then the sound of cracking glass woke her.

Allison stiffened, afraid to move. She held her breath and tried to quiet her pounding heart. She listened for footsteps, an opening door, any kind of movement. Nothing. She glanced down at the foot of the bed where Lancelot still slept peacefully. It must have been part of the dream, she thought. If there had been any kind of noise, the cat would have been under the bed in a blink.

She had to make sure, though. She walked through

all the rooms, telephone in hand. She turned on every light, checked every window, every lock and bolt. All was secure.

She slid slowly under the covers again, careful not to disturb Lancelot. She was too jittery to go right back to sleep. Portions of the dream kept darting through her mind. She wondered why Gil was in so many scenes. Fred had cleared him of suspicion. Why couldn't she accept that?

She needed to examine something in the dream more closely. She tried to remember each part that concerned Gil: the dog, the car, his mother. "That's it," she said to the sleeping cat. "Fred said his parents were killed in an accident. But Gil told me he visited his mother, and that his dad bought him the car. How could that be? And Fred said Gil was from a middle-class family, but apparently he told Martha he came from a poor background. Why would Gil belittle himself? It doesn't make sense." Allison turned over and pulled her comforter up. I need to trust Fred on this one, she thought, and quit making Gil into a bogeyman. As sleep crept over her once again, she murmured, "But where did he get the money for that car?"

SIXTEEN

BETWEEN CLASSES the next day, Allison saw Martha and Tim come out of Mr. Forster's office. She hurried down the hall and caught up with them as they were leaving. "Something new on the school break-in?" She couldn't imagine any other reason why they would be here.

Tim shook his head. Martha did the explaining. "We're following the money trail. Buck Franklin gave us the names of all the people he could remember who bought items at the art show. He'd already deposited everything in the bank, and we know who paid by check from the deposit slip. Now we're talking to those who paid in cash. He knows he took in at least three one-hundred dollar bills, but he couldn't remember who from. We're checking out each buyer. Your Mr. Forster was one of them."

Allison shook her head and rolled her eyes. "He's not my Mr. Forster. I just happen to work for the man. He's not really an art lover either, but he thinks he has to put in an appearance to set an example for the students. What did he buy?"

Martha consulted her notes. "A print of the old

school before the gym was built. He said he was going to hang it in his den at home. Forty bucks. Said he paid with two twenties."

"You sound tired," Allison said. "Have many to go?"

Martha nodded. "Too many."

"We have found one person who paid with a hundred," Tim chimed in, "but he said he got it when he cashed his paycheck at the bank. The bank teller confirms that she did give him some big bills, so it's not likely he's our culprit."

"But anyone could say they got the bill at the bank or the drug store or anywhere," Allison said. "I don't see that you're going to accomplish anything."

"Maybe not," Tim said. "I guess we're just trying to lay some groundwork for the Secret Service."

"As far as that goes," Martha said to Allison. "We only have your word that you got the bill at the art show. Are you sure you don't want to fess up?"

Allison waved her hand at the two law officers. "Get out of here and go track down some real criminals. I've got to get back to my classroom before my students tear it apart." She wheeled around as a playful shriek echoed down the hall. She called back to the retreating uniforms, "And you think you have a tough job."

ALLISON SKIPPED SCHOOL on Thursday, a rare event. She decided she had to have some time to think. She called into the office as soon as she thought Mr. Forster's secretary would be in. When she answered,

Allison gave the excuse of a cold coming on and that she was going back to bed.

"That's the smart thing to do," the secretary said. "You don't need to be here spreading your germs around. I'll get a substitute for you. I'm sure Susan Webb will be available. She likes all the work she can get."

Allison thanked her, made sure Lancelot had food and water and crawled back under the covers. But bed didn't last long. Allison always thought better on her feet. She climbed into her gray sweats, searched the closet floor until she found her oldest Nike Airs, grabbed her parka, and headed out the door. She took a deep breath and smiled at the emerging day. It had rained during the night, and the grass shimmered in the sun. The stinging cold of the past week had dissipated, the sky was translucent, and somewhere in the distance Allison heard the plaintive *coo-coo-oo* of a mourning dove. Maybe Fred was right, she thought. Maybe spring *is* just around the corner. One could never be sure in the upper South.

She drove toward the river north of town. The city fathers had recently dedicated Riverview Park there, complete with walking trails. One trail started at a majestic magnolia tree, its branches cascading toward the ground, its dark green leaves glistening. No other cars stood in the parking area. She hadn't expected any. Allison felt deliciously naughty spending a school-day morning all by herself.

She walked at a brisk pace, swinging her arms,

breathing in rhythm with her steps. A fragile peace slowly seeped into her body, into her mind. She was in the "now" where past and future didn't exist. She was one with the trees, the birds, the trail, the fluffy clouds. Her lips and her heart smiled.

Her euphoric state lasted less than five minutes.

A short way down the path, she realized she was not alone in the park. A man's footprints stared boldly at her from the damp earth. They had to be fresh prints because the recent rain would have washed away any others.

An uneasy feeling teased her brain, heightened her senses. She could hear Fred's warning words a few days ago, "There's a dangerous man loose in your lovely little town, and he doesn't mind killing people."

Allison hesitated and glanced back at her nice, safe car. Then she took a deep breath and scolded herself for being silly. Murderers don't take morning walks in parks, she reasoned. They're too busy hiding, or scheming, or hightailing it out of town. The footprints must belong to a nature lover, or another troubled soul who needs space to think. Allison plunged ahead. The trail wound around some gray boulders, through a stand of river birch trees, and at one point, followed a narrow peninsula and out into the stream. Allison drank in the winter beauty, the invigorating coolness of the air, tried to forget about the person on the path ahead.

Rounding a sharp bend, Allison caught a quick glimpse of the man who belonged to the footprints.

All she could tell about him before he disappeared behind a clump of bushes was that he was tall and thin and dressed in black. Again she hesitated. She was scared.

Her thoughts swirled around. Should she run to her car? Get out of there as fast as she could? But what if she had Leroy's partner within sight? Maybe she could get a glance at his face without him seeing her. She couldn't let this chance get away.

She quickened her steps, hurried around a curve in the trail. The man in black was crouching down by a large rock. Allison paused and felt the tension ebb out of her body. She recognized the long black overcoat. She'd seen it the previous Saturday evening. She came closer. "Good morning, Professor Keyes."

The man kept his head bent toward the ground and made no move to get up. The tail of his coat was covered in mud, as were his black gloves. He seemed to be digging for something beneath the rock. Allison bent toward the kneeling man and asked rather hesitantly, "Do you need some help?"

"Yes, I rather do." He turned to face her. He swiped at his shaggy eyebrows which looked determined to curtain his cornflower blue eyes. "I'm trying to dig out this clump of hepaticas without disturbing their roots. These are the first I've seen this year." He leaned back so Allison could view the slender thin stems. "They're the first woodland flowers that bloom here in the spring. Now is a good time to transplant them—before they bud."

"I see," Allison said. "Maybe if I push back on the rock you can get to them easier."

The man squinted at her and shoved back his canvas hat. "Didn't you tell me you were still teaching? What are you doing out today?"

Allison laughed. "Playing hooky. But don't tell anybody."

"You're secret's safe with me. Let's see if we can get these little beauties out of here."

Allison placed both hands on the top of the rock and started pushing.

The rock tipped up enough for the professor to dig underneath and free the hepatica's delicate root system. "Easy now. Hold it steady." Allison held steady, Professor Keyes tugged, the flowers came loose. "There we are." He held the plant up to the sunlight. "You'll love your new home in my rock garden." He nodded that Allison could turn loose. She straightened up and offered the old man a hand. He accepted and she heard a distinct creak as his knees unbent. "This may be the last year I'll be able to roam the woods and roadsides, so I'm moving my beloved flora to my backyard. My legs are giving out on me. I just pray that my senses don't. As long as I can see and touch and smell my friends, I'll be happy."

Allison knew the professor was a widower who lived alone in a nearby development. "You walk here often?"

"As often as this decrepit body can make it. I usually walk as far as the mill, but I think I'd better head back home now and get these in the ground. I don't want the roots to dry out." He started to leave and then turned back to Allison. "It might not be a good idea for you to walk up that way. There's been something funny going on at Valley Mill."

"What do you mean, funny?" Allison immediately pictured Leroy dangling dead from a monster machine.

"I saw the picture in the paper of that man they said was killed in an accident. I recognized him at once."

"You knew Leroy Hastings?" Allison couldn't imagine Professor Keyes and Leroy being acquaintances.

"I didn't know his name, but I used to see him on Friday evenings when I walked up that way. He and a young fellow would be out back of the mill loading a barrel on an old pickup truck. I didn't think anything about it the first few times, but then I got to wondering if maybe they were doing some illegal dumping of chemicals. I was afraid they might be polluting our beautiful river, and I couldn't stand by and let that happen."

The wheels in Allison's mind were spinning faster than a runaway top. Barrels? Chemicals? Young fellow? She stared questioningly at the old professor. "What did you do?"

"I went right up to them and demanded to know what was in the barrel. The older man, that Mr. Hastings, said it wasn't any of my business. And he wanted to know why I was sticking my nose in where it didn't belong."

"What did you tell him?"

"I told him I was Professor Keyes, that I lived on the other side of the park, and that I wasn't going to stand for any pollution in the area. Then the young man spoke up. He was nice and polite. He explained that it was just detergent and that he was taking it to the landfill. He said they couldn't dispose of it in their plant's plumbing because the suds weren't good for the septic system. He even opened the lid and let me look in. I stuck my finger in and, sure enough, it was just soapy water. So I didn't say anything else about it."

Allison knew Leroy always worked late on Friday afternoons, but she didn't know anyone worked with him. In fact, Leroy had bragged to her one day that he was a one-man maintenance crew. "Would you know the young man if you saw him again?" she asked the professor.

Professor Keyes shrugged. "I just saw him up close that one time. He had a stocking cap pulled down over part of his face. It was a pretty cold day." He closed his eyes a moment and then nodded. "But yes, I believe I might recognize him. Especially his voice."

"His voice?"

The professor bobbed his head in certainty. "When he spoke to me that day, his voice was soft and pleasant. Let's see, that was either two or three weeks ago. But when they were arguing this past Saturday, he used curse words I hadn't heard since my navy days. I'll never forget *that* voice." Professor Keyes looked at the flowers in his hand which were quickly wilting. "I've got to go."

Allison wasn't about to let this font of information get away. She felt an excitement in her bones. Maybe the professor could lead them to Leroy's partner. "I'll walk with you," she said. "I'm pretty good at digging. I'll help you plant your little friends."

"That's so kind of you. I've had a hard time with a shovel lately."

As they walked back down the trail, Allison said, "So you saw Mr. Hastings and this young man on Saturday?"

Professor Keyes nodded.

"At the mill?"

The professor nodded again. "That's right. I thought it was strange. I'd never seen anybody at the mill on weekends before. I didn't walk last Friday, so I don't know if they were there or not, but they were loading the barrel Saturday when I walked by. I'm sure they didn't see me; they were too busy arguing."

"What were they arguing about?"

"I couldn't make that out. The older man, Mr. Hastings, was shaking his finger at the young fellow. And the young man was ranting and raving and cussing. When they got the barrel loaded, Mr. Hastings jumped in the truck and drove off, and I think he shouted something like, 'I'll be back.'"

Allison was puzzled. "I've never seen Mr. Hastings drive a pickup."

"Oh, I think it must be a company truck. It stayed parked in back of the mill most of the time. It's there now. At least it was yesterday. The employees' cars are parked out in front."

"Did you see Mr. Hastings again after he drove off ?"

"No. The paper said that he probably died Sunday. I didn't walk on Sunday so I don't know what went on at the mill. But I tell you something strange is going on there."

"You're right, Professor Keyes," Allison said, "and you need to tell the police exactly what you've told me. It may help them in their investigation. After we've re-planted the hepatica, I can take you to police headquarters and you can talk to Detective Steve Pritchard."

The professor's eyebrows lifted in surprise. "Is Steve in on this? I know Steve. We've eaten lunch together at the Burger Shack. Fine fellow. I'd be glad to talk to him. He knows how to treat people." Professor Keyes's eyes grew misty. "He lets me rattle on about my flowers. I know I'm just a boring old man, but Steve always pretends to be interested in my hobby."

Allison smiled at the old professor. He looked so tired and frail. It's sad, she thought, for such a masterful mind to outlast its body. They had reached his yard and Professor Keyes collapsed in a lawn chair. "You rest," she said, "and I'll dig. Just tell me where and how deep."

Allison dug and planted according to the professor's instructions. When she finished, he thanked her, and begged off going to the police station. "I really need to go in and rest some. Maybe Steve could come by here later to talk to me."

Allison looked at him with concern. He seemed so tired, so fragile. She decided he needed his rest now more than he needed to talk to the police.

SEVENTEEN

ALLISON LEFT THE PROFESSOR, walked back to the park to get her car, and drove to the police station. Steve was surprised to see her, and she explained about her day off. She then told him how she'd run into Professor Keyes, and his story of events at Valley Mill.

"Professor Keyes? I see him fairly often at the Burger Shack. He's always talking about wild flowers."

"That's right. He remembers you, also, said you were a fine fellow. Of course, I had to agree with him." Allison gave Steve a big grin. She was beginning to think that all detectives were pretty fine fellows. She could hardly wait to call Fred tonight with this latest news.

"I've enjoyed talking to the professor," Steve said, "or rather listening to him as he explained natural habitats, endangered species and his concern for the river. He's a real scholar and a gentleman."

"So do you want to go back and talk to him now?"

"I think I'd better go to the mill first to see if I can find out who Leroy's mysterious helper was. Everyone I talked to there said Leroy worked alone and had no close friends at the mill." Steve tilted back in his chair and studied the notes he'd taken. "I especially want to find out why Leroy was hauling away soapy water."

Steve rose and put on his jacket and motioned Allison to the door. She was hoping he would ask her to accompany him. He didn't. As he was taking the front steps two at a time, she called after him, "You'll let me know what happens?"

He stopped in mid-step and turned to face her. "Now, Miss Nosy, why would I do that?"

Allison checked his face for a trace of a smile and decided he was doing his best to hold it back. "Because," she said, "I'm an interested party, because I brought you some important information, because…." Her mind went blank for moment, then she blurted out defiantly, "And because I'm going to help you solve this case."

"Well, when you put it that way, I'll certainly keep you informed. In fact, I'll stop by your house later and you can go with me to visit the professor." Allison nodded in satisfaction and headed home to her coffeepot.

HER PHONE RANG a couple of hours later. "We'll catch the professor this afternoon," Steve said. "I need to check some other things, then I'll fill you in on all I know."

Allison spent the intervening time once again dissecting, analyzing, memorizing the cryptic calendar entries. But her mind gyrated from the coded figures to thoughts of soapy water, to a man in black, to poor

Malvina's summer cruise, and then back to C-V and F-M. Caffeine and chocolate kept her psyche in high gear, but did little to cut through the chaos. She gladly abandoned the task when she saw Steve pull up into her carport. Tim unfolded his long legs, stepped out, and held the door for her. Allison hesitated. "I don't want to take your seat, Tim. I can sit in back."

Tim shook his head. "No, Mrs. Aldridge. You sit up front with Steve. I'm going to sit in back and take lessons."

"Lessons?" Allison frowned. "What are you talking about?"

"Steve said you were going to solve this case for us, and I don't want to miss a thing."

Allison glared at the detective behind the wheel, plopped down on the seat next to him and slammed the door. She vacillated between being angry and laughing at her own expense. Her schoolmarm experience prevailed. Allison had learned early in her career that making fun of herself was a sure way to win students' respect. She favored Steve with her biggest smile. "Excuse me a minute while I pull my master detective foot from my mouth. Right now my brain feels like mush, and I couldn't solve two plus two without using my calculator." She paused just long enough for her chagrin to appear valid and then added, "I really do appreciate you allowing a civilian to tag along on official police work. It's a great learning experience." Allison ignored a chuckle from the backseat and gave Steve a look which could only be described as awestruck.

Steve cleared his throat and sat up straighter. "Well now, let me update you on our latest findings." Allison's head bobbed up and down in anticipation. "No one at the mill can identify Leroy's companion. Crandall swears that Leroy always worked alone. He has no idea where the soapy solution came from, or why they would be dumping it in the landfill. He says the plant just makes and prints fabrics. They don't wash them. This was corroborated by the workers in the mill. Stitson, the payroll clerk, said Leroy was authorized to work overtime on Fridays to make sure everything was shut down and secure for the weekend. But Leroy did it by himself. Stitson even showed me the time cards. No one else ever worked late on Friday or any other day. So we have to assume the person Professor Keyes saw didn't work at Valley Mill."

"Unless someone is lying," Tim said.

"Time cards don't lie," Steve insisted. "What do you think, Mrs. A.?"

But Allison wasn't thinking about time cards. Her mind had taken a sharp detour a few sentences back. "Stitson? Wally Stitson? Wally works at the mill?"

"Yeah," Steve nodded. "I said he's the payroll clerk. You know him?"

"Yes. That is, he's a former student, and I saw him just recently at the art show." Allison rubbed her lips as she tried to sort out her thoughts. "So that explains the picture of him and Mr. Crandall together. They must have been discussing something about work."

Steve gave her a puzzled look and Tim asked, "What picture?"

Allison explained about the picture she'd seen in the *Holliston Journal*. "Somehow I can't picture Wally working in an office. He seemed too Bohemian for that."

Steve raised his eyebrows. "The word 'office' may be a little overblown for the lean-to room Stitson works in. It's more like a cubby hole stuffed with computers, copying machines and files. He has a dilapidated desk, a battered metal safe stacked with filthy coffee cups, and walls covered with pin-ups from a Sports Illustrated Swimsuit Edition." Steve glanced at Tim in the backseat. "Of course, it was Tim who explained to me where the pictures came from."

"Of course," Allison murmured. Tim made no comment.

"And," Steve went on, "since there's no dress code at the Valley Mill, Stitson can be as Bohemian as he likes. He seems to know his job, though, and Crandall praised him for cutting out unwarranted overtime. He's got everybody except the boss and himself on time cards. Stitson comes and goes at lot, running errands and stuff for Crandall. But everybody else has to punch in and out and have prior approval for overtime. It seems the textile business has gotten rather wobbly the past few years. They can't compete against foreign plants with cheaper labor costs. In fact, Crandall confirmed a rumor I'd heard about the mill moving to

Mexico. He said the plant here will be shut down in a few months."

"Yes," Allison said, "I heard that rumor, too. It's going to be hard on a lot of people."

They neared the subdivision where Professor Keyes lived and Steve slowed the car. He turned to Allison for instructions. "I'm not sure which house he lives in."

"Around the next corner, middle of the block." She examined the houses as they passed. "This used to be a nice neighborhood, but it's going downhill fast. A lot of the houses seem to be empty."

"They are," Tim agreed. "The younger people are moving out near the new golf course. That leaves just the old duffers hanging on here."

Allison indicated the professor's house, and Steve parked in front. The three walked up on the porch. Steve rang the doorbell, and they waited. No sound came from within. He knocked several times. No answer.

"I'll check the back," Tim volunteered. In a few moments, Allison heard him shout, "It's open. Better hurry, Steve." Steve hurried. He took the three porch steps in one stride and sprinted to the backyard. Allison was close behind. Tim stepped back to reveal splinters of wood scattered down the steps, the screen door dangling by one hinge, and the other door halfway open. "I haven't touched anything," Tim assured the detective.

"Good." Steve pushed the door gently with his right

foot. It swung wide. The officers drew their guns, and Steve motioned Allison away from the door. Steve entered the house first, followed closely by Tim. Allison crouched down behind a bayberry bush under the kitchen window.

She wanted to run through the house, calling out to Professor Keyes, to find the old man, and be assured of his safety. Instead she followed the two men with her eyes as they slowly and quietly made their way through the kitchen, across the hall, and then disappeared into another room. Allison strained to hear any sounds coming from the room. A TV commercial jingle floated out the back door and she recognized the voice of a History Channel commentator. She gave a little sigh of relief. Everything's fine, she thought. Professor Keyes is just relaxing and reliving our nation's past. He probably didn't hear the doorbell or the knocking on the front door. The back screen door could have been broken for some time. She waited for Steve to call out to her, to tell her it was all right to come in. But no such word came.

They'd probably forgotten all about her, she fumed. Poor thanks for leading them to a key witness. A chill wind made her shiver. They were in there questioning the professor while she stood out in the cold. Well, she could do something about that.

Allison stalked in through the open door, intent on not being left out. She strolled down the hall following the TV voices, and thought it strange that she didn't hear the men's voices. She approached the room at the end of the hall where Tim's back blocked the doorway. She started to tap him on the shoulder when she glanced past him. That was when she saw the professor sprawled on the floor.

EIGHTEEN

ALLISON CLAPPED HER HAND over her mouth to smother a scream. Her eyes flinched at the scene before her. Professor Keyes was lying face up at the foot of his recliner. A trickle of blood made one of his eyebrows resemble a brush smeared with red paint. The color coursed down his sunken cheek, came to rest on the collar of his gray wool sweater. Under one hand was a copy of *Guide to Wildflowers.*

Steve knelt beside the old man. "Damn," he choked, as he felt for a pulse. He sat back on his heels, swiped the back of his hand across his eyes and shook his head. "Damn, I should have come right back here. He hasn't been dead but an hour, maybe two. It's my fault. I shouldn't have gone back to the station first."

Allison dropped to the floor. She wanted to take the old man in her arms and beg for his forgiveness. "No. It's my fault. All my fault. He trusted me with his story, and I let him down. I went off and left him alone." Allison knew she couldn't touch the professor and maybe disturb some evidence, so she put her head on Steve's arm and sobbed. "Who could hurt such a kind old man?"

Steve sniffed, trying in vain to hold back his own tears. "Believe me, we're going to find whoever did this. I swear to God we'll find him." Allison wasn't surprised at Steve losing his professional objectivity. For all his mischief in school, he'd been a caring child. She recalled the day one of the younger students had taken a bad fall during football practice. The coach had simply told the boy to go back to the gym and call his mother. Steve had insisted on going with him, and he ended up carrying his injured friend to the first-aid room. Allison decided the prerequisite for being a good cop was to have a tender heart.

Steve blew his nose. "At least this narrows our range of suspects. It has to be someone at the mill, or someone connected with it. I didn't say anything about the professor, or a possible witness while I was there, but the culprit must have figured it out."

"And then he scooted over here," Tim added, "to make sure Professor Keyes didn't talk anymore. Struck him on the head a couple of times. Probably didn't take much to kill him. The old fellow was pretty frail anyway. He may not have heard his assailant break in with the TV on."

Steve asked Tim to take Allison home while he waited for the crime lab people. "Go home and get some rest," he instructed her. "You look drained. I'll check with you later."

She gave him a grateful smile. "Thanks. I guess I need a little time to sort through my emotions. Things are happening too fast." Allison followed Tim out of the room, careful not to touch anything.

On the way home, Allison's thoughts swirled around like a Kansas tornado. She tried to remember every detail of Professor Keyes's description of the young man with Leroy. It wasn't much: thin face, stocking cap, black jacket and gloves—a description that could have matched the person who broke into her house.

The professor said the man could be nice and polite when necessary, but he could also cuss like a sailor. She turned to Tim and tried to keep her voice causal. "Why did Steve go back to the police station today when he left the mill?"

Tim shrugged. "I guess he wanted a report on what the rest of us had found. Martha, Gil, and I were following up leads on the counterfeit money."

"Find anything?"

"Not really. The bank reported a twenty that had come in from Judd's Gas Station. Amos Judd had no idea who zapped him with it. But he was plenty mad. Martha checked with all the surrounding banks. Charlotte is the only city that's been hit a lot. Gil went to see the Arts Council treasurer again but didn't come up with any other helpful info."

"Buck Franklin's a good businessman," Allison said, "and has a good memory for names and faces. I'm sure he gave all the information he could."

"Franklin a friend of yours?" Tim asked.

"Yes. I think a lot of him. He does a lot for the community."

They drove in silence for a few minutes. Allison

wanted to steer the conversation back to what each of the officers were doing earlier, but she didn't want to be too obvious. "So-o," she said, "after Steve heard your reports, he told the three of you that Professor Keyes could identify Leroy's partner?"

"Well, he said he hoped the professor would be of some help. He showed us the report he'd made out about your encounter with Professor Keyes." Allison recalled Steve filling out the report: the professor's name, address and the gist of their conversation.

"And that's when you two came by to get me?"

Tim turned his attention from the street long enough to give Allison a questioning look. "Not right then. We went to lunch first. Why?"

"I was just trying to get the time frame straight," Allison said. "I know, I know. I'm trying to play detective again. So humor me. You, Steve, Gil, and Martha went to lunch together. How long did it take you? It was nearly one-thirty when you picked me up."

Tim pulled into Allison's carport and turned to face her. "You are undoubtedly the snoopiest woman I've met since I left home. I could never hide anything from my mother, and you're just about as bad."

Allison shrugged. "Why would you want to hide anything from me—or from your mother?"

"Okay, I give up. Steve and Martha and I went to *Pizza Palace* for lunch. We all ordered the special. It was busy. We waited for thirty minutes and took another thirty to eat. Martha went back to the office, and we came over here."

"Where did you lose Gil?"

"As we started out to lunch, Gil said he was feeling sick—said he couldn't eat anything. He did look a little pale, so Steve told him to go on home. His shift was about finished anyway. We've all been putting in a lot of overtime, and Gil hasn't really been feeling well lately." Tim paused. "Anything else you want to know?"

"No, I guess not. Thanks for the ride."

"You're welcome." Tim rolled down the passenger window as Allison got out. "But let us do the detective work." Allison waved as he backed out of her drive.

Should she have told Tim about her suspicions of Gil? But what if she was wrong? She couldn't accuse somebody of murder unless she was sure. But what if she was right? "I'll call Steve later and tell him," she said to herself. "Then it'll be out of my hands."

Allison reached into her parka pocket for the door key. Her fingers found not only her own key, but another one caught in the corner seam. She pulled it out and puzzled over it. Recognition came slowly. It was the key Malvina had given her years earlier, which Allison had handed to Gil less than a week ago. She vaguely remembered Gil returning it, and that she had dropped it in her pocket. She contemplated the key as she gazed at the now vacant house next door. The police had searched the house thoroughly and found no clues. Why did she have this urge to do her own search? Tim's last words rang in her head. Allison knew he was right.

She needed to leave the detective work to the police. There was no reason for her to think she could find something they'd overlooked.

She slipped the Hastings' key back into her parka and inserted her own key in her own lock. She knew she should go into her house, fix a cup of coffee, and collapse on the couch. But her mind recoiled. Allison's snooping hormones rioted. She had to have one more look at her neighbors' house. Malvina might have left some clue which only Allison would recognize. Or bumbling Leroy may have written cryptic messages on something other than a calendar. She exchanged keys and headed next door.

NINETEEN

As she walked toward the Hastings' house, Allison thought of Malvina's sister. Faye had called her Monday evening after she'd been told of Leroy's death. "Leroy's accident was terrible," Faye said, "but at least we know he's not suffering or in pain. I wish I could be sure of the same with Malvina."

Allison understood. It was better to know the worst than to know nothing. Faye had come to her sister's house, straightened up a bit, done up the unwashed dishes, and gone back home to await further word. There had been no further word, and it was now a week since Malvina disappeared. Allison wished she could find something to comfort Faye, some clue to help unlock the mystery.

She let herself in the Hastings' back door. She tried to survey the room as if she had never been there before. If she were a new detective on the scene, where would she start? The desk in the corner of the kitchen seemed a logical place. There wasn't much there. She found a stack of paid medical bills, an address book with less than a dozen names, note cards with pictures of sunsets and sailboats, and a photograph album. The back page of the telephone book was neatly filled with the numbers of Malvina's doctors and relatives. A new calendar, replacing the one given to Allison, hung on the wall above the desk. The only date marked on it was Malvina's January doctor appointment.

Allison sat in the desk chair and tried to conjure up her neighbor. "Speak to me, Malvina. Did you leave a message for me, for anyone?"

She wandered through the silent rooms, flipped through magazines, looked under newspapers and behind pictures. She knew her quest was futile and foolish. She'd read her share of the mystics, the New Age Gurus, the teachings of God's guidance. She wanted to believe it all. She wanted to believe if she just had enough faith, then some answer, some sign, would come to her. She wanted to believe, but reality kept interfering. "I'm sorry, Malvina. I can't hear you. There's nothing I can do here. I've got to go home." She cracked open the back door. A gust of wind tore at her coat. Then she heard a noise that stopped her.

A jingle, faint but distinct, came from somewhere in the room. Not exactly a bell or a wind chime, but definitely a soft clink or clank, a tiny tinkle. Her eyes probed every inch of the walls, the ceiling, the furniture. The room was silent. Allison sniffed back tears, leaned against the wall by the phone, and shook her head in despair.

Clink, clank. The sound came from behind her head. She turned, looked, caught her breath. Three keys hung on a hook by the phone. "So this is your message,

Malvina." Each key was tagged with its identity: *storage shed, extra car key, cabin.*

Tim had checked out the storage shed that first night. So it has to be the cabin, Allison thought. But what cabin?

She tossed the key up and down in her hand, trying to remember when she'd heard mention of a cabin. It came to her when she saw the mounted antlers above the mantle. Malvina had told her about Leroy killing a deer while at the company cabin. She'd said that Mr. Crandall gave keys to some of his employees so they could use the cabin for hunting and fishing. Malvina had even shown Allison a picture of Leroy in front of the cabin with the deer strung up by its hind legs.

Allison lunged toward the photograph album on the desk. Her mind searched for other references to the cabin as her fingers searched for the picture. Both succeeded. She found the snapshot of Leroy at the rustic cabin, and recalled Malvina saying that the cabin was north of town next to the river. It should be simple enough, she thought, to follow the river upstream until she found it. She had no idea what she would find there, but instinct told her she *had* to follow this clue.

She crammed the picture and the cabin key in her pocket, carefully locked the Hastings' door, and hurried home. She glanced at her watch. Only a couple of hours of daylight left, but she reasoned, it shouldn't take long to get there.

She unlocked her door, grabbed her car keys and

scooted back out. As she was backing the car out of her drive, she realized she should let Steve or someone else at the police station know where she was going. She rejected the idea immediately. "They'll tell me to stay home and behave myself," she grumbled as she careened down the street. "But I can't stay home. Malvina wants me to check out the cabin, and I'm going to do it."

Allison knew the roads well. Years of hauling her own and neighborhood kids to scout camps, wilderness adventures, and river rafting proved their worth. She drove confidently north, winding down roads seldom used and little known. Glimpses of the Valley River appeared through naked branches. She slowed as the road became narrower, the houses fewer. For the first time she wondered whether she would recognize the cabin if she saw it. After a particularly long stretch of road without seeing a building of any kind, she began to worry that she might have missed it. "It might be back in the woods, can't be seen from the road," she muttered. "And maybe this was a crazy idea. I shouldn't have come alone. What was I thinking? Oh, why didn't I get a cell phone as the kids urged me to do? But no, smart me, I said I didn't need to be in touch with the world every minute. Well, I surely wish I were in touch with some of the world right now."

Allison's conversation with herself was cut short when she rounded a curve and the cabin came into view. Her excitement outweighed her qualms as she pulled into the empty drive.

The cabin looked like something built out of a Lincoln Log Set: square, squat, dark green roof. She parked next to the brick chimney, opened the car door, and hesitated. She surveyed her surroundings. Afternoon shadows bathed the cabin in shades of gray and mauve. It was eerily quiet until a low wind wailed through shivering pine needles. All the ghost and horror stories she'd ever heard cascaded through her head, paralyzing her body, jangling every nerve. She took a deep breath and reminded herself why she was here. A clue. She desperately needed a clue. And it might be in this cabin. She scanned the area for signs of life, and convinced herself there weren't any. The cabin had to be empty. She overcame her fear, slid out of the car, threw back her shoulders, and marched to the door. The key fit. The door opened. Allison entered.

Her eyes flitted nervously from side to side, front to back; her feet reluctantly followed. Allison explored the entire space. It didn't take long. The cabin contained only one large room with a kitchen area and a tiny bathroom. It was empty, but obviously it had been used within the past few days. Baked beans left on a plate were dried out, but not yet rocklike; bacon in the refrigerator smelled old, but not rancid; rotting food in the trash can emitted a disgusting stench. Two cots, one on either side of the room, had been slept in, their blankets pushed back. A pillow lay on the floor next to a hunting magazine. The floor was dirty, with dried mud on top of dust, but it was impossible to make out any distinct footprints. Dishes in the sink seemed to be in pairs. There were two plates on top of two soup bowls, two cups, and two glasses.

But who had been here? Were the two people Malvina and her captor? Was it possible?

Allison picked up the dingy pillow and examined it carefully as if it could tell her whose head had most recently rested on it. Nothing. She grabbed a magazine from the floor. Its cover featured a largemouth bass dangling in mid-air with a barbed hook through his lower mouth. That's me, she thought, dangling hopelessly in search of a kidnapper, a murderer. She flipped angrily though the pages until she came to where part of one page had been torn away. A big, black motorcycle gleamed in what was left of the advertisement. The rider had been removed. Allison wondered if there could be any significance to that, or had someone simply ripped the page indiscriminately?

She let her gaze wander around the room, noted the fishing gear stacked in one corner, a shelf with cards and poker chips, a hunting vest with bullets still in their little slots, a flashlight hanging from a nail by the door. The flashlight reminded her of how dark the room was becoming. Little of the late afternoon sun managed to sneak into the cabin. She pulled out one of the chairs by the table, sat down and pondered her next move.

Had it been foolish of her to come here? She'd found nothing to explain Malvina's disappearance or Leroy's death or the professor's killing. And Allison knew she had no business trespassing on private property. Furthermore, she thought, she'd better get out before it got really dark.

She started to get up when she saw something under one of the cots—something which looked familiar. It was the color of fallen acorns, crumpled like an empty sack. Allison held her breath as she sprinted to the cot, dropped to her knees, and grappled in the dark space. Her hands touched a soft worsted fabric. She pulled at it, but it was bunched between the legs of the cot.

With one heave, she pushed the cot sideways, tugged at the cloth, and jerked out the object. It was Malvina's winter coat!

Allison's thoughts played leapfrog. Malvina had been here. Where was she now? Who was with her? Why did she leave her coat? Allison hugged the coat to her chest, buried her face in the smooth lining, smelled Malvina's *Sunflowers* perfume. "Talk to me, Malvina," she cried out. "Tell me where you are. Tell me who took you away." Allison held the coat out in front of her. It was in good shape, no rips, no blood. That's good, she thought. Maybe Malvina hadn't been hurt.

A piece of paper fluttered from one pocket onto the floor. Allison picked it up. It was the missing rider from the magazine's motorcycle. The rider's face had been punched out and all that was left was a thin man dressed all in black. Allison desperately turned the other pockets inside out. "I need more than that, Malvina. A name! I need a name!"

Allison started to shiver. The temperature in the room was dropping faster than the setting sun. "I have to get out of here," she cried to the empty room. "I've got to get to a phone. Got to call Steve." She scrunched Malvina's coat under her arm, and swiped away tears of frustration.

A scraping noise prompted Allison to lift her eyes from the coat to the door. It was slowly, menacingly opening. She smothered a scream as her eyes stared at the emerging black clad figure. The young man entered and silently closed the door.

The coat slipped from Allison's hands as she backed away in terror. "You!" she wailed.

TWENTY

"HEY, CALM DOWN, Mrs. Aldridge. I just followed you to see if you needed any help." Gil Watts smiled and stepped toward Allison. "I lost you when I had to stop and get gas, but I thought I'd keep on driving north in case I spotted you again. And, sure enough, I saw your car in front of the cabin. Whose place is this?"

"You know whose place this is. Stay away from me. I'm warning you. I can defend myself. I'm not weak and sickly like Malvina. I don't know what you've done with her, but you won't get away with it!"

Gil shook his head. "I don't know what you're talking about. I'm one of the good guys. Remember?"

Allison edged toward the kitchen. She remembered seeing several knives near the sink. She had to get her hands on something, anything, to defend herself. She had no illusions that she could be a match for the young policeman, but she certainly was going to try. And she intended to get some answers. "Why did you come back here?"

"I've never been here before, Mrs. Aldridge. I told you I followed you here." Gil spread his hands out as if in supplication. "You've got to believe me. I'm on your side. I was on my way home when I saw you run out of the Hastings' house and drive away. I was afraid you might be heading for trouble. Now suppose you tell me what *you're* doing here."

Allison's voice wavered as she pointed to the brown heap on the floor. "That's Malvina's coat. Where did you take her? And how did you get mixed up with Leroy?"

"I tell you I don't know what you're talking about." Gil took a step closer and bent over to pick up the coat.

Allison reached behind her, felt an object on the bar, grabbed it, raised it up to shoulder height, and aimed it at Gil's head. It missed.

Gil looked up in surprise as a ketchup bottle skidded across the linoleum. "Aww, come on, Mrs. A. You've got me all wrong. Now, be a good girl and stop throwing things at me." He grabbed her arm as she tried to maneuver past him toward the door. "Trust me. I'm not going to hurt you. I just want to find out what's going on."

Allison jerked and grappled and scratched. "Let go of me," she gasped.

Gil held her tightly. "Not until you calm down. Then maybe we can talk sense."

Allison didn't hear the door open again. Apparently, neither did Gil. But they both spun around when it slammed shut. "Wally Stitson!" Allison cried out and breathed a sigh of relief. "I don't know what angel brought you, but thank goodness you're here. I need help."

Wally didn't respond. He stood still, hands in his pockets, hooded eyes flitting from his former teacher to the young policeman. He shook his head slowly, and just as slowly pulled out his right black-gloved hand. In the hand he clenched a small revolver. "Yes, teacher, you need help." His words were low and husky and slurred. "We all need help."

Allison pushed back against Gil. Wild thoughts slammed against her brain. Why did Wally have a gun? What was he doing here? Her thoughts were gone in a nanosecond. There was no time for Q & A. It didn't matter. Here was her protector—her savior. She pulled away from Gil's grasp and rushed toward Wally.

"Keep him covered," she cried out, pointing to Gil. "He's a kidnapper and a murderer."

Wally raised the gun and pointed it at Gil as Allison came closer.

Then with a sad smile he inched the gun's aim away from the young man and toward the oncoming woman.

"No!" Gil shouted.

The gun exploded just as Gil knocked Allison to the floor and fell on top of her.

Allison lay on the cold linoleum trying to figure out what had happened. She wasn't hurt, but she was pinned to the floor. Why was Gil holding her down? And who had Wally shot at? She wiggled, sat halfway up, and reached her hands out to push Gil away. She felt something sickeningly warm and slimy. She managed to turn her head just enough to see her hands covered with blood. Then she saw that the blood was oozing from Gil's chest.

Before she had a chance to react, the sound of a second shot echoed through the room at the same time it tore across her skull.

Allison collapsed back, her head hitting the floor with a loud crack.

She lay there stunned, unable to move. Her body was numb; she had no feeling of pain, no feeling at all. She didn't know if her eyes were open or shut; she saw only blackness. But she could hear. Strange, she thought, to be able to hear such mundane sounds as scuffling and gurgling when she was obviously dying.

She couldn't untangle her thoughts. Wally had come to save her. Or had he? Why was Gil bleeding on her? And what was running down her forehead? She reached her hand up and felt more blood. Was it Gil's or her own? It was too much for her brain to process. She tried to blot out everything, but the sounds kept bringing her back. She heard footsteps. She heard cursing. Then she heard a thunderous crash, a muted popping noise, running feet, and a banging door.

Moments later she realized she retained another one of her senses. She could smell. And what she smelled was kerosene.

Gradually Allison perceived that she was not dying. With a mighty effort, she cracked open her eyes, turned her head to the right, and saw Gil's face, ghastly white with splotches of spattered blood. "Oh, my God!"

It all became clear to her—Gil had taken the bullet meant for her. And then there had been another shot. And that one had hit her. Her fingers explored her left temple that had started throbbing. She cringed as she felt the wet, gooey mess.

She tried to put her own condition out of her mind and turned back to Gil. He's dead, she thought. He'd saved her life, and now he's dead. "I'm sorry, Gil," she cried. "I was wrong. I'm so sorry." Allison raised her head and laid it against Gil's cheek. She felt a quiver. Had it come from Gil, or her own shaking body?

She took a gulp of air to calm herself, and then *all* of her senses kicked in. She heard Gil moan, she tasted her own blood dripping inside her mouth. She smelled the kerosene fumes. She saw licks of flames creeping toward them. She felt heat filling the cold cabin. Her mind sent her one urgent message after another. Gil's alive. The cabin's on fire. We've got to get out.

She quickly pulled Gil over on his side so she could slide out from under him. As she did, blood spurted from his chest onto the floor, spreading like spilled paint. She reached in her jacket pocket for her scarf and stuffed it into Gil's gaping wound.

She looked over to see where the flames and heat were coming from. Wally's last demonic act had been to knock over the heater, rupturing the kerosene line. Either he had thrown a match, or the fuel had been ignited by the pilot light. The stove was on the opposite side of the room, but she knew it would explode in a matter of minutes. Then the cabin would be engulfed in flames. She and Gil would be two charred bodies. At least, that's what Wally must have planned.

Allison had a different idea. "I've got to get you out of here, Gil. You saved my life. Now it's my turn."

She sent up a quick prayer, crawled to her knees, pushed herself to a sitting position, waited until the world stopped spinning. She stood up and grabbed Gil's arms. She stretched them above his head and started pulling. He didn't move. "For a skinny fellow, you're mighty heavy," she panted. The streaks of flame were now licking the table legs and singeing the edge of a blanket. Again Allison wrestled with Gil's arms but managed to move him only a few inches. She kicked Malvina's coat out of her path and bent down for another try. Sweat was trickling down her face mixing with tears of frustration. Blood was seeping through the packing in Gil's chest. The heater gave an ominous shudder. "Oh, God, help us. Gil doesn't deserve to die like this. He's got his whole life in front of him. Help me get him out."

She grasped her hands around his, bent her knees, and turned her eyes away from his ashen face. A button on Gil's jacket caught on Malvina's discarded coat. Allison leaned over to disentangle the two coats and recognized that this might be the answer to her prayer. She spread out Malvina's coat next to Gil, knelt down by his side, pulled him toward her, and slid the long coat under his head and shoulders. As she turned Gil on his back, she noticed the flames getting closer, the room hotter. She was surprised that the stove hadn't already exploded. She hurriedly buttoned the coat across Gil's chest below his armpits. Then gripping the coat's sleeves, she pulled with all her strength. The coat slid across the worn linoleum like a sled on hard-packed snow. Allison shoved the door open and skidded Gil through the opening.

Once outside, she wondered if she could get to one of the cars. They were parked at the side of the cabin next to the chimney. Even in her dazed condition, she realized she had to move in the opposite direction— away from where the fire had started. She jerked her makeshift litter around and headed toward a clump of trees she saw in the distance. Before she got very far, the explosion she'd been expecting came.

The sound was deafening. Allison closed her eyes, threw her body over Gil to protect him from falling debris. She lay motionless until the noise abated and then cautiously opened her eyes to survey the destruction. The entire cabin had erupted like an angry volcano. Sparks leapt to the top of the pine trees, and light from the shooting flames rivaled the setting sun.

Allison turned her attention back to Gil. She snaked her precious cargo across the open field away from the fire. If she could get to the trees they might be safe until help arrived. But *would* help come? Would the fire and smoke be seen by someone and be reported? It would be completely dark soon and then the flames would be even more visible. But who would see them? Did anyone live in this deserted area? When she was driving up here, she hadn't seen a house within miles of the cabin.

She reached the woods as another explosion rattled the trees. Allison slipped down to the ground, curled her legs under her, placed Gil's head on her lap and stroked his face. "That was either your car or mine," she said to the unconscious police officer. She slid her fingers to his temple and felt his pulse—faint and irregular. She unbuttoned the coat to check the bleeding. It seemed to have slowed.

Her son's face danced before her eyes as she studied the young man. "You've got to live, Gil. I'd like you to meet Dave. You two could be friends. You could play Ping-Pong with him in our basement. Remember you asked me about the Ping-Pong table? I know now you were just trying to be a good cop. But I didn't trust you. How could I have been such a fool? You've got to give me a chance to make this up to you."

Allison sniffed back tears, leaned against a fallen tree trunk, and thought how nice it would be to take a nap. "But I can't," she said, jerking upright, "I've got to do something." Her eyes rested on the burning cabin. Soon there would be nothing left, and the fire would burn itself out. What if no one had heard the explosions? What if the flames had not be seen above the treetops?

Allison eased herself from under Gil's head, and tucked Malvina's coat gently around him. "I'm going to have to leave you," she whispered. "I'm going to walk until I find help." As she propped his head up higher, her knees bumped into something rigid in his pants pocket. She reached to pull it out of the way so he wouldn't be lying on it, and her hand grasped a cell phone. Of course, she thought, Gil would carry a phone. Why hadn't that crossed her mind?

She stood up, flipped the phone open, and was dismayed to find that she was out of range. So she would have to walk after all. Hopefully it wouldn't be far. She leaned against a tree trunk to steady her swimming head and wobbly legs, then started toward the road.

As she walked, she tried to figure out how Wally Stitson fit into the puzzle. He was, no doubt, Leroy's elusive partner. She was sure now that he was the intruder she'd seen in her own house. He must have left the art show and gone straight there. And he must have killed Professor Keyes. But what were he and Leroy involved in that was worth killing for?

"Enough of that," she told herself. "The only thing that matters now is getting help for Gil." She was still out of range. She kept walking, positive that the phone would soon come alive. After several minutes and no response from the cell phone, she was torn between going on or returning to Gil. She decided she had to go back. She couldn't leave him alone any longer.

She was exhausted and her legs were trembling by the time she reached the woods. It was nearly dark now and Allison wasn't sure just where she'd left Gil. She pushed her way through some trees and the branches slapped at her head. She put her hands on her forehead to push her hair back. Her left hand found only bloody matted stubble. She'd forgotten about her own wound until that moment. Now her legs buckled under her as her mind visualized where Wally had meant the bullet to go. It was the closest she'd ever come to fainting. She slumped to the ground. But instead of landing on leaves and twigs, her hands felt cool damp soil. In the last of the fading daylight, Allison could make out a long, slim mound of dirt. Tears streamed down her cheeks. "So this is what he did to you, Malvina."

TWENTY-ONE

THE DARKNESS DEEPENED. Allison knelt by the grave. In the distance she heard a siren, low and far away. At first she took it to be a distant train whistle and thought of Wally at the art show saying he'd like to get on a train and ride forever. Maybe that's what he's doing this very minute, she thought.

The siren's wail became louder, closer. Allison jerked up her head. Someone had seen the fire. Help was coming. She forced herself to stand, decided her legs were working again, and hobbled over to Gil. His lips were blue, his breathing barely perceptible. She bent over and took his limp hands in hers. They were like two blocks of ice. "Hang in there," she said. "Help is on the way."

She headed for the clearing. A fire truck swerved and came to a stop in front of the cabin. Men jumped out, started unwinding a hose. Allison staggered toward them, waving her arms and shouting. "Get an ambulance! A man's been shot! Call the police!" She was no stranger to issuing orders, and she immediately got their attention. "I need help over here. Hurry."

The men dropped the hose. One of the firemen

motioned the other two to go with her, and he shouted back, "I'll call for the sheriff and ambulance."

Allison nodded. "Then pull your truck up. We need the light." She turned and ran, leading the way back to the woods and to Gil.

In the glare from the truck's headlights, Gil's face took on a ghostly pallor. Allison did her best to keep back tears as one of the men checked Gil's pulse. He shook his head. "Nothing we can do. The ambulance will be here soon."

He turned to Allison. "What happened?"

She told her story in bits and pieces. The men said they knew about the missing person. "You mean she was held here in this cabin?"

"Yes. And I'm sure that's her grave over there." Allison pointed to the mound of dirt. "They've got to stop Wally before he kills someone else. Set up road blocks. Check the trains."

"The sheriff's deputies are on their way. This is outside the city limits, so the county sheriff has jurisdiction here."

"But you've got to call the Holliston police as well." She pointed to Gil. "He's a city policeman, and he's been shot in the line of duty. Call Steve Pritchard. He's the detective on the case."

The fireman nodded and made his way to the truck. When he came back, he assured Allison that both county and city officers would soon arrive.

He looked toward the cabin. "The fire's about burned

itself out. Looks like the cabin is gone, along with any evidence it might've contained.

"The cars?" Allison asked. "They were parked by the cabin."

He shook his head. "I doubt there's much left of them."

Other sirens shrilled through the darkness. The ambulance arrived before the police. Allison watched as the EMTs changed the packing in Gil's wound, started intravenous fluids, administered oxygen. They wasted no time getting him ready for transport and relaying information back to the hospital.

One of the medics insisted that Allison, too, had to go to the emergency room and be checked out.

"I know. And I will. But first I have to wait and talk to the police. Steve will take me to the hospital."

"All right. I'll tell them to be expecting you." He jumped in the back with Gil and the ambulance took off.

Two patrol cars shrieked up the road as the ambulance sped down. They drove up next to the fire truck. Martha bounded out of the lead car before it came to a complete halt.

The firemen motioned to where Allison sat vigil by the recently dug grave. Martha ran over and embraced her.

Allison collapsed in the comforting arms. "Gil saved my life," she wept. "He took the bullet meant for me."

Martha hugged her. "Tim's gone to the hospital. He'll keep us informed about Gil's condition." Martha backed away as Steve came up but whispered to her, "Gil's going to make it. He's tougher than a junkyard dog."

Steve introduced Allison to two officers from the sheriff's department. After they all heard the essence of her account, Steve gently took her elbow and led her away from the woods. The others started the grim task of digging, using one of their car's headlights to illuminate their task.

"We got a description of Stitson's car from the DMV and put out a bulletin. He won't get far," Steve assured her. "The State Police will probably pick him up in just a little bit."

Allison began to shiver uncontrollably. She didn't know if it was the cold night air or a reaction to her horrible day. The firemen moved their truck back to the cabin site and were hosing down the embers. One of them came up and suggested she get into the cab of the truck. "There's a blanket in there and I'll turn the heater on." She nodded thankfully.

As the warmth enveloped her, she leaned her head back and closed her eyes. But there was no rest for her. Faces danced behind her eyelids: sweet Professor Keyes, brave Gil Watts, poor Malvina and Leroy, malicious Wally Stitson. And then the only face that could bring her any comfort, that of her distant friend, Fred Sawyer. "Oh, how I wish you were here, Fred," she murmured. "You'd be able to make some sense out of all this." Her head throbbed, her limbs ached, her heart wept.

She didn't know how long she'd sat there when Steve tapped on the door and opened it slowly. The cab's overhead light etched deep shadows under his eyes and turned his skin sickly yellow. Steve took Allison's hand as he confirmed the grave's occupant. "I'm sure it's Malvina, although we'll have to wait for positive identification. Looks like she's been dead several days, no obvious cause. We'll see what the medical examiner has to say."

Allison swiped tears with her free hand. "It really doesn't matter now. Does it? Wally killed Malvina and the professor, probably Leroy, and now maybe Gil." She squeezed Steve's hand, and her voice broke. "How can one person be so evil?"

Steve shook his head. "I doubt I'll ever understand the criminal mind. Maybe Fred can help answer that question." He attempted a smile. "I called him. He's on his way. I figured you could use a friend. But right now, we've got to get you checked out at the hospital."

TIM MET THEM as they entered the emergency room. "Gil's in surgery. No word yet."

Steve asked, "Were you able to get in touch with his sister?"

"She's on her way from Raleigh. Should be here soon."

Allison allowed herself to be led to an examining room, to be poked and prodded, to have part of her head shaved, salved and bandaged, to have her eyes, her memory, and her orientation tested. "Close call," the doctor commented. "But no serious damage. You must have a guardian angel."

"I do," Allison answered, "and he's in surgery right now."

Steve came in as the doctor finished. "Can she go home now?"

"As long as someone is with her."

"You can be sure of that." Steve helped her off the examining table and guided her to the door.

Allison held back. "I want to wait until Gil gets out of surgery. I've got to be sure he's okay."

"We'll keep you informed about his condition," Steve assured her, "but right now Martha is going to take you home. By the way, Fred just called. He's about thirty minutes away. Martha will stay until he gets there."

Allison yielded to Steve's authority. She really didn't think she'd be able to hold her head up much longer anyway. The doctor had given her a pain pill. Not only had it quieted the throbbing in her head, but it also was lulling her to sleep. She collapsed in the passenger seat of the patrol car, turned glazed eyes toward Martha and slurred, "Home, James."

BY THE TIME they reached her house, Allison's hazy mind was cavorting through an episode of *The Twilight Zone*. She was battling weird monsters papered with counterfeit money, swatting black spiders with a rolled up calendar, and rescuing wildflowers from a river of soapy water. It was all Martha could do to extricate her ward from the car and deposit her on the den sofa. "Whew! That must have been some pill Doc gave you."

"It's all connected. Don't you see?" Allison slurred. "It's all connected. It's all there. We just have to figure out how it fits."

"Sure, but don't worry about it now. Just rest."

FRED ARRIVED with a screech of tires, a slamming door, and a knock that echoed through the carport. Martha let him in and motioned to the den. Fred stood in the doorway, his gaze fastened on Allison on the couch. She looked so small, so fragile, so wounded. He crossed the room, and took her hands. He kissed her bandage. He kissed her cheek. He kissed her lips.

And then he scolded her. "Allison, you promised me you wouldn't do any snooping."

"I know." Her lips began to quiver. "But the pot wasn't simmering enough."

"And you had to stoke the fire."

"I guess that was what happened." She buried her head in her hands and let loose a torrent of tears. Fred didn't try to stop her. He just lifted her head to his shoulder and let her cry it out.

"It's all so terrible," she bawled. "Malvina in that cold grave. Sweet, kind Professor Keyes, who never hurt anybody. And Leroy." Allison lifted her head. "Leroy was into something he had no business doing, but still, he didn't deserve to die like that."

Fred pulled her closer and said nothing. Later they would talk, he thought, but right now Allison needed to vent her anguish.

"And Gil." The name brought more tears. "He saved my life. You told me he was clean, but I didn't believe you. I accused him of killing Malvina. Oh, Fred, do you think he'll ever forgive me?"

It was Martha who answered the question. "He'll forgive you. He'll understand. We'll go see him tomorrow and explain." Martha sat down at the end of the couch and clenched her hands. "I just hope he can forgive me. I never treated him right."

Allison's sobbing subsided to a low moan. Fred grabbed a handful of tissues, wiped her eyes and made her blow her nose. "Now, partner, Martha is going to get you undressed and into bed. Then she's going to leave, and I'm going to sit here and keep watch over you. Tomorrow we'll talk. Okay?"

"Okay." Martha half led, half carried her into the bedroom.

As soon as the door was shut, Fred made two long-distance calls. Allison's children needed to know what had happened. He found their dorm numbers on the back of the telephone book. When he talked to both Connie and Dave, he minimized her ordeal and injury, but suggested that they cut classes the next day, and be here for their mother. She was going to need all the emotional support she could get.

They didn't require any urging. "I'm on my way," Connie said. "I'll drive by and get Dave. We'll be there in a few hours."

TWENTY-TWO

ALLISON AWOKE WITH the first shafts of daylight stealing through partially open blinds. Her mind instantly kicked in where it had left off the evening before. But now the message was clear. It all had to do with what Fred had called, "funny money." Leroy and Wally were counterfeiters. Somehow they made the money at the mill and washed it on Friday afternoons so the new bills would appear to be old. That was the soapy water Professor Keyes had seen. She still didn't know where the calendar fit in, but it would come. Maybe Wally was already in custody. Maybe he had confessed to everything. Maybe the nightmare was over.

Allison sat up to call Fred when she saw a pair of men's feet encased in dingy white socks sticking out from the rocking chair by her bed. Her first thought was that Fred didn't use enough bleach in his wash. The second thought was she'd never seen Fred wear white socks. Her eyes followed the socks up to long-legged baggy jeans, a Myrtle Beach tee shirt and a baby face covered with fine stubble. "Dave?"

The feet jerked, the face came alive. He covered the distance between the chair and the bed with one stride, bent down and gave her a gentle squeeze. "Hey, Mom," he said. Then with a devilish grin, he added, "What's for breakfast?"

She returned his hug. "It's so good to see you. But what are you doing here? You're not due home until Spring Break." She hugged her son again. "But I'm so glad you're here."

"I had to come and see what trouble my old lady had gotten herself into now. With that bandage around your head it looks like you're auditioning for *The Mummy Walks Again*."

"This thing?" Allison brushed the gauze and tape that topped her head. "As soon as I can get to a mirror, this is coming off. Believe me, it's just a scratch."

"A scratch that could have killed you." Connie came into the room waving a pot holder. "Fred told us what happened. Off chasing a killer by yourself! Mom, what were you thinking?"

"I wasn't chasing anybody. I was trying to find a clue about what happened to Malvina. And I sure didn't know the killer was chasing me." Allison gazed at her children and tears filled her eyes. They were so beautiful. Connie with her long, dark hair pulled back in a pony tail, her brow furrowed in worry over her errant mother. Playful, boyish Dave, love showing through his foolishness. "It's so good to have you both here. It's almost worth getting shot at to have my babies home again."

Connie leaned over the bed and embraced her. "You

can thank Fred for that. He was so worried about you that he demanded we come home." Connie stood back and gave her mother a loving gaze. "And it's a good thing he did call. You wouldn't have told us anything about it. You think you're so self-sufficient."

"I don't feel self-sufficient at the moment. In fact, I may need help just getting out of this bed. And I do have to get up. I've got to tell Fred and Steve what I figured out. I think I've solved the puzzle. At least, part of it. Where's Fred now?"

"Trying to wake up. He slept on the couch. I tried to get him to go to bed in Dave's room, but he insisted on staying close by you." Connie shoved the pot holder at Dave. "Check on the bacon while I see if I can make Mom halfway presentable. I don't want Fred to see her looking like a haunted-house refugee."

Connie reached down, helped her mother out of bed, and headed her toward the bathroom. "You need a good bath and a miracle make-up job."

"I can't look all that bad," Allison said. One look in the mirror convinced her otherwise. What little hair was showing stuck out in spikes, her left eye was nearly swollen shut and a sickly greenish-yellow hue was creeping down her cheek. "Good gosh!" she cried. "Did anybody get the license number of the truck that hit me?"

Before she let Connie start to work on her, Allison insisted she call the school office to get a substitute teacher again. "I can't just not show up. But don't tell her anything. Only that I need another day off. I don't want the whole school buzzing about my little escapade."

The do-over took several minutes, but when Allison emerged from her room, Dave whistled and Fred smiled appreciatively. Connie had replaced the big bandage with a narrow strip of gauze and tape, back-combed her mother's hair to nearly cover it and applied plenty of makeup.

Fred reached for her hand. "You look great. You know, you really had me worried last night." Then he lowered his voice as his lips brushed hers. "In fact, you look good enough to eat."

"Hey," Dave called out. "There's no time for smooching. Breakfast is served."

Silence reigned around the table as they bowed their heads. In a wavering voice Allison said the blessing. "We thank you God …"

Allison was surprised by her ravenous hunger. Mystery and murder were put on hold while she began to devour the crisp bacon, cheese omelet, and buttered grits.

In the middle of the meal, the telephone rang. Dave jumped up to answer it and handed the phone to Fred. "Steve wants to talk to you."

Three forks hung in suspension as Allison, Dave, and Connie listened to Fred's end of the conversation. All they heard was, "ah ha," followed by, "that's good," and, "I see."

Fred laid down the phone and quietly returned to his seat.

"What?" Dave asked.

"Gil's off the critical list," Fred said and beamed a smile around the table. "We can see him later today."

Allison folded her hands and closed her eyes for a moment. "Thank God. Then he's going to be all right?"

"Seems like." Fred dabbed strawberry jelly on his toast before continuing. "No sign of Wally yet. But they'll find him."

When everyone finished eating, Connie shooed the others into the den while she cleared the table. Then she crumpled a piece of leftover bacon for Lancelot and joined them. "The dishes can wait while Mom tells us what she figured out about the mystery."

All eyes turned to Allison. Dave scooted the desk chair closer. "Wait a minute," he said. "First Connie and I need to get up to speed with all that's happened so far. Fred told us a little last night, but he was too worried about you to go into everything."

"You're right," Allison said. "You need to know it all. Fred, would do the honors?"

Fred nodded. He told of the break-ins, Malvina going missing, the deaths of Leroy and Professor Keyes, the funny money floating around, the cryptic calendar, and ended with what Steve had told him about the happenings at the cabin. Dave and Connie listened in rapt silence except for outbursts of "Omigawd!"

"Okay, Mom," Dave said, "now tell us everything you've figured out."

"Well, I haven't actually figured out anything. But what I think is that everything is connected with counterfeit money." She explained her theory about Leroy and Wally making the funny money at the mill and washing it to make it look old. "Fred, remember Professor Keys said he saw some soapy water behind the mill."

"Sure did. Makes sense to me. So that's the game they were into. And somehow Malvina got in their way. But how does the calendar fit it?"

Dave stood up and stretched. "How about letting me have a crack at it? Where is this mysterious calendar?"

"The copy is in my desk, top drawer." Allison's eyes misted as she watched her eager young son. He approached the calendar as he did every problem—total concentration and complete confidence. All three observed him silently, expectantly.

He turned his back to them. "I can't think with all of you staring at me. Have some more coffee and leave me alone for a few minutes."

Connie headed back to the kitchen. "I'll load the dishwasher while you think, little brother. And you'd better come up with something by the time I get through."

Fred wanted Allison to lie down on the sofa, but she insisted the recliner would suit her better. She rested her head back, cradling her coffee mug in her right hand. Fred pulled a chair up close and held her left hand.

Allison zoned out. She wished life could stay this way, safe and warm. No crime, no danger, no crazy calendars.

Dave interrupted her paradise with a triumphant,

"Aha." He swung around and grinned. "You're right, Mom. The money trail starts here. I've deciphered Leroy's pitiful code."

Allison slowly returned the recliner into the upright position and leaned forward. Fred jumped up, crossed the room and draped himself over Dave's shoulder. Connie hurried in from the kitchen. Dave stood and gave a slight bow.

"All right already," Connie said. "Are you going to tell us or do we have to beg you?"

"I'm telling. I'm telling." He waved a sheet of the calendar in the air. "It's really very simple. And Mom is absolutely right. It is about the counterfeit money. You remember there are two numbers in each note. Therefore I concluded the first number represents the denomination of a bill; the second is the total number of bills to be printed. For instance…." He pointed to the entry in March: *F-M 20/500.* "Here the counterfeit order was for 500 twenty-dollar bills to the tune of ten thousand dollars."

Fred nodded. "Makes sense. And what about the initials?"

"That's the recipient, the person who gets the funny money. There are only two sets of initials so Leroy only had two customers." Dave flipped over a couple of pages. "In May C-V got ten thousand dollars in hundreds while F-M got another ten thousand in twenties." Dave tossed the calendar in the air with an Olympic-size smile. "Simple."

Fred nodded his head in admiration. "I think you

have the numbers correct because all the counterfeits reported have been either twenties or hundreds. But your mother said the letters couldn't be a person's initials because of the hyphen."

Connie picked the calendar up and stared at the entries. "So we'll have to study on that some more. But what I can't figure out is why would Leroy write down incriminating information in such a public place?"

"I think Steve had the answer for that," Allison said. "He thought that writing it on the calendar made Leroy feel clever and important."

"And," Dave added, "it gave him a record of transactions in case the other guys tried to bail out and leave Leroy in a sinking ship. But I don't see where Wally fits into all this."

"I'm not sure." Allison tried to recall all she knew of her former student. "Wally was smart, artistic and imaginative. But he had a dark side. He used to play what he called 'practical jokes' on his classmates, but they were really pretty mean tricks. I never met his parents, which means they never came to PTA meetings or student conferences. And in my mind, no parental involvement in school translates into little parental caring at home."

"Wally was a year or two older than I was," Connie said, "but I remember him, probably because he did have a reputation for meanness. He would draw ugly pictures of some of the girls and leave them on their desks. He was not a nice person."

Allison nodded. "I suspect that it was Wally who

made the counterfeit bills. Maybe Leroy only got involved because he had a maintenance room where he worked alone and unsupervised. Leroy may have been able to mix up the right solution needed to age the bills."

Dave jumped back into the conversation. "So do the police think Wally killed Leroy? Or is it still listed officially as an accident?"

"I don't know what the police think," Allison said, "but I think it was Wally."

"Me too," Dave agreed. "But I can't come up with a reason."

Connie turned her attention to Fred and asked, "What do *you* think, Fred? After all, *you're* the real detective here."

Fred grinned at the serious, dark-haired beauty sitting next to him and saw a picture of Allison twenty years earlier. "Thank you for that acknowledgment, Connie. I'm glad somebody remembered." He held up his hand to block any response from either Allison or Dave. "As a matter of fact I do have a theory. I never met the Hastings, but according to Allison they were a devoted couple. When Malvina disappeared, I think Leroy figured out that Wally had to be involved. He accused Wally and, of course, Wally denied it. Remember the argument between them that Professor Keyes told Allison about?"

The others nodded and Fred continued. "Wally was probably afraid of what Leroy would do if he found out the truth. But before Wally could deal with that, he still needed to get the calendar back. When that failed, he felt the walls closing in. If Malvina wasn't found, he knew the police would question Leroy further, then Leroy would crack, and their neat little scheme would fall apart.

"Wally's only chance was to silence Leroy. He either arranged to meet him at the mill on Sunday or they met by accident. One or both of them may have been trying to get rid of evidence. At any rate, Wally killed Leroy and made it look like an accident. He'd probably already buried Malvina, so he thought he was home free."

"But where does Professor Keyes come in?" Connie asked.

Fred turned to Allison. "Did I understand you to say that Steve went to the mill Monday to find out who was helping Leroy load the barrels of soapy solution?"

"Yes," Allison said. "He didn't mention anything about the professor at the mill, but then I guess he didn't have to."

"That's right. Wally remembered him from Saturday. He knew the professor had witnessed the quarrel between him and Leroy. He had to get rid of the old man. As so often happens, one murder leads to another and another." Fred's voice trailed off as he remembered that Wally had intended Allison to be his next victim.

Allison broke the silence. "Gil said he followed me

after he'd seen me next door. I'd guess Wally was cruising around, saw me too, and followed both of us."

"Or perhaps, Mom," Dave said, "he was going back to the cabin to clean up any evidence that tied him to Malvina. He just happened to arrive after you and Gil did."

"Maybe. I just wish they'd find him." Allison shuddered. "Then we could put this mess behind us."

Connie shook her head. "It's going to take more than finding Wally. We also have to find F-M and C-V." She picked up the calendar one more time. "And if little brother can figure out the numbers, I ought to be able to decipher the letters."

Dave clapped. "Yeah, yeah. Go for it, Sis."

"Well, there can't be many names that start with V in Holliston. So let's try the phone book. I know Mom ruled the letters out as being a person's initials, but we have to start someplace. The phone book might give us something to go on."

"I think it's a good idea," Dave said, grabbing paper and pencil. "You read and I'll write."

Allison sat with her hands folded in front of her and beamed at her children. Just like their old mama, she thought, bursting with pride. A sign flashed through her mind, *Aldridge Family Detective Agency. Reasonable Rates. Satisfaction Guaranteed.*

Connie's voice interrupted the vision. "Vaccardi, Vaga Dance Studio, Valentine, Valeri, Valley Mills, Vallingham, Van Horne, Value City, Vangolf, Van

Patten, Victory Gym, Vince, Vukovinch and Vuncannon Hosiery Outlet."

Dave counted the names. "That's nine individuals and five businesses. I'd forgotten that in small towns they put residences and business numbers together. They don't do that in bigger cities."

"I told you there were advantages to living in a small town," Allison said. "It's better than having to look in two or three different places for information."

Connie frowned. "But what information do we have? I know some of those families, and you probably know all of them, Mom. Are any of them the criminal type?"

"Not in my wildest dreams."

"So we're exactly nowhere. Some detective I am." Before Connie could berate herself any longer, the telephone rang. Allison grabbed it and answered.

"Allison," the voice on the other end said, "Martha here. I'm on my way to the hospital to see Gil. I thought you might like to meet me there. They took him out of ICU this morning."

TWENTY-THREE

THEY ALL DECIDED TO GO. Martha met them in the lobby and Allison proudly introduced her children. "So pleased to meet you," Martha said. "Did your mother tell you we added more people to the force just to try to keep her out of trouble?"

Dave shook Martha's hand and laughed. "No. But I'm not surprised. We've had a problem with her for years."

Connie put her arm around Fred's shoulder. "We even called in troops from out of town to keep her in line, but it hasn't helped much. She still wants to play detective."

"It isn't really my fault, you know," Allison said. "You have to blame it on Aunt Dolphinia."

Connie and Dave stared at their mother. "Old Aunt Dolphy?" Connie said. "You mean our great-aunt who lives in a nursing home?"

"Yes. Because when I was four or five, she lived down the road from us and I spent many hours sitting by her side as she read to me."

"So?" Dave held his hands out, imploring an explanation.

"So," Allison grinned as she readied her punch line,

"Aunt Dolphy always read me the adventures of Agatha Christie's Miss Marple. Ever since then, she's been my role model."

Fred howled. Martha bent over in spasms of laughter. Connie shook her head, and Dave threw up his hands.

The laughter drew the attention of the desk clerk who put her right index finger to her pursed lips in the universal sign meaning *Hush!*

GIL WAS SITTING UP in bed, an intravenous line in one arm, oxygen tubing in his nostrils, and a smirk on his face. As his visitors trailed into the room, Gil's cheery voice met them. "It'll take more than a bullet to get rid of me."

Allison hurried to his bed, bent over the side rail and took his hand. "You look wonderful! I'm so sorry."

"You're sorry I look wonderful?"

"You know what I mean." Allison slapped him gently on the hand. "I'm sorry I suspected you. You really are one of the good guys. I can't thank you enough for what you did."

"That goes for me too, Buddy." Fred stepped forward for a man-to-man handshake.

"And us," Dave added as he and Connie stepped forward. "We haven't met, but I'm Dave, Mrs. Aldridge's favorite son, and this gorgeous gal is Connie, my sister. She got the beauty in the family, but, fortunately, I got the brains."

Connie reached up and took Gil's hand. "Of course, Mom has both of us beat. Thanks for being there for her."

Martha tip-toed to the other side of the bed. She waited until Gil turned his face in her direction. "I just wanted you to know that I'm mighty proud of you— everybody at the station is proud of you."

Gil nodded. "Thanks." His eyes seemed to mist momentarily, then the corners wrinkled up to match the corners of his mouth. "Does that mean I'll get a bigger badge?"

"No," Martha said, "but if your head gets much bigger, we'll give you a bigger cap."

A nurse came into the room pushing a dressing cart. "I don't know how all of you got in here at one time, but you'll have to leave now. When I'm finished changing his dressing, two of you can come back. But only two."

"We were leaving anyway," Fred assured the nurse. The five of them scooted out the door, waving their goodbyes.

"I'll be back," Allison managed before the curtain swept Gil away.

He called out to them. "My sister, Eleanor, went to get some coffee. If she's out there, say 'Hey' to her."

They headed down the hall to the elevator and were met by a female replica of Gil. The girl was older, but had the same reddish-blond hair, pale skin, and freckles peeking out from under her make-up. Introductions were quickly made with Eleanor balancing coffee in one hand, and shaking each of their hands with the other.

Fred led them to chairs in a mini-waiting room. "I guess you know your brother is a hero," he said. "Gil saved Allison's life."

"I know. Detective Pritchard told me what happened." Eleanor took a quick sip from her cup. "Of course, he's always been a hero to me. Even though he's my kid brother, I've tended to lean on him. Especially after our parents were killed."

Allison leaned forward. "That must have been awfully hard on both of you."

"It was. But Gil helped me through it. He kept telling me that they weren't really gone, that as long as we remembered their love and their faith they would always be with us."

Allison had to readjust her thinking about Gil again. Not only was he brave and self-sacrificing, he was also tender and sensitive. It certainly didn't jibe with the brash, irritating personality he had exhibited earlier.

Eleanor seemed to read her thoughts. "Sometimes he makes jokes or tells outrageous stories to hide his soft side, but he's really very sweet. He bought the Eldorado with part of his share of the insurance money. Our father sold Cadillacs, and Gil said it made him feel close to Dad to have that car. He plans to get another one just like it. Gil gave the rest of his money to me so I could open up a boutique. I always wanted my own business. We decided to keep the home place and rent it out. Gil keeps it in good repair. He says every time he goes down to check on the house, it's like visiting the folks."

Allison nodded. "He told me he hadn't a chance to get back to visit lately."

"No. He's been pretty busy. He loves police work." Eleanor shuddered. "I hope he's not going to make a habit of catching bullets."

WHEN THEY GOT BACK HOME, Connie insisted that her mother lie down. "I'll call you when lunch is ready."

"Or when you hear any news," Allison said. "Martha promised to call the minute they had any information about Wally. Or if Steve calls or…."

"Or if the end of the world is announced. Yes, I'll let you know."

Allison didn't get much rest. The phone rang shortly after she'd hit the bed. She was up in a flash and back in the den. Dave answered the phone, handed it to Fred. "Steve. He's wants to talk to you."

Fred snatched the phone, gave a couple of grunts and an "Oh-oh."

All three Aldridges hunched around Fred trying to make sense out of his responses. He ended the conversation with, "So there's another one out there."

When Fred hung up the phone, Dave threw out the question, "Another what out where?"

Fred closed his eyes, shook his head, and said

wearily, "Another killer in your little town. They found Wally. He'd been shot—several times."

Connie fell back on the couch. "Is this nightmare never going to end?"

Allison rubbed trembling fingers along her bandage and recalled her near escape from death. But there was no sense of relief or triumph over the death of her assailant. She felt only a deep sadness for the wasted life and talent. "Where did they find him?"

"By the river," Fred said. "He must have met someone in the park. His car was behind a clump of trees. His body was further upstream. Apparently, the killer tried to shove the body in the water, but it caught on a tree limb."

"But who?" Dave said. "We know Wally probably killed the others. But who killed Wally?"

"The answer has to be on the calendar," Connie said. "We've got to decipher what the letters mean."

Allison made her way to the recliner, propped up her feet, and stared at the painting over her desk. Maybe it could give her a breakthrough, a new way of looking at things. Maybe the vivid colors erupting from the chaos was enlightenment. She tried to clear her mind of preconceived ideas, to open herself up to guidance, to wisdom. Perhaps the letters were initials, but not of first and last names. They might indicate cities, events, businesses. Businesses! Allison slammed the recliner to its upright position and winced as her head bounced back and forth. "Oooh, I forgot about my poor head."

Fred gave her a sympathetic gaze. "You really should get some rest."

"No time now. Got to think." She glanced over to her daughter studying the calendar. "Connie, hand it to me."

Connie looked up in surprise, but did as she was told. "Got an idea?"

Allison nodded. "Now get the telephone book again and read me the names of the businesses that start with V."

Connie thumbed through the telephone book and found the Vs. "Vaga Dance Studio, Valley Mills, Value City, Victory Gym, Vuncannon Hosiery Outlet."

"And which of those businesses is connected to the counterfeit money?" Allison asked the three people in front of her.

Dave and Connie answered in unison, "Valley Mills."

Fred nodded his head like a wobble doll. "Of course. But what does the C stand for?"

Allison reached for the phone. "We've got to call Steve and tell him to find Crandall."

"Crandall?" Fred stared at her without comprehension.

"Crandall?" Dave's voice echoed Fred's incredulity.

"Crandall!" Connie gazed openmouthed at her mother. "Of course!" She ran over and gave her a hug. "Crandall is CV! How could we have missed it?"

Allison grinned. "Crandall-Valley. It was right in

front of us all the time. Everything that's happened has been connected with the Valley Mill and Crandall is the owner. That's got to be it!" She started punching numbers on the phone.

"Hey, wait just a minute," Fred said. "You can't point a finger at this Crandall guy just because his initial happens to match Leroy's gobbledygook."

Dave and Connie stood behind their mother as if in a face-off against Fred, the detective. He laughed and shrugged his shoulders. "Go ahead and call. There's no way I'm going to go up against the whole Aldridge family."

Tim took the call, sounded skeptical, but said he'd pass it on to Steve.

"So," Dave said, "while we're waiting for the cops to capture the master criminal, let's eat." Connie emptied the refrigerator and Dave concocted a baloney, cucumber and onion sandwich slathered with mustard. "Nothing like solving a crime to whet your appetite."

But halfway through lunch, Allison began to have doubts. "What if we're mistaken about Crandall?" she said. "After all, I was wrong about Gil. Rufus Crandall is a respected businessman, a member of the Chamber of Commerce, and lives in one of the best neighborhoods in town. How could he be involved in counterfeiting and murder?" Allison looked up from her plate of cottage cheese and realized no one was paying much attention. She raised her voice. "And furthermore, Mrs. Crandall always donates prizes for our school's Fall

Festival. She's a very nice lady." Fred looked at her oddly and Connie shrugged.

Dave scratched his head. "But, Mom, it was Crandall's mill, Crandall's employees, Crandall's cabin. He had to be involved. There's no question in my mind."

Allison nodded. "Of course. It has to be him." Dave's confidence made her feel better.

"And as soon as I finish off these chocolate chip cookies," he said, "we'll tackle the next assignment—nailing down F-M. Where did you put the telephone book, Connie?"

Connie reached for the book and flipped through it. "But, Dave, there's three pages of Fs and five of Ms. How can we dig through all of them?"

"We don't have to. It's simple, Sis." Dave spoke as if he were explaining long division to a third grader. "Since C was Crandall and V was Valley Mills then F must be a man's name and M would signify the business that man is in." He grabbed paper and pencil. "Read me the first business or company under M."

Connie ran her finger down the page. "Matt's Video."

"Good. Now we have to find if anybody with the last name of F works there."

"Dave," Connie said with just a hint of sarcasm, "You know who works there. Matt Webber. He's the owner, the proprietor, the bookkeeper—the whole shebang. He may hire some high school kids on the weekend, but otherwise he's it."

"Okay. Okay," Dave said. "I was just using that as an example." He turned to Fred who was watching the pair with intense interest. "What do you think, Fred? Am I on the right track?"

"Maybe so," Fred said. "I'm just sorry I didn't think of it."

Dave appealed to the other person in the room. "Mom?"

Allison shook her head and tore her mind away from Rufus Crandall. "I'm sorry, Dave. What were you saying?" Dave explained his strategy one more time and his mother agreed it was worth a try. "We just have to be careful," she cautioned, "not to jump to conclusions." *As I already have,* she thought.

Dave decided they would make a list of the businesses and then if they didn't know the owners or managers, they would simply call and ask. He even wrote out a script to explain why they were asking. After a few calls, Connie had her role down pat. "Hello. This is the *Holliston Journal* calling. We're compiling a list of businesses to appear in an upcoming issue. It will mean some free advertising for your company. I need to verify who owns the business and the top managers. Could you please give me that information?" All the business people were glad to comply.

Fred gave the kids his cell phone to use so they wouldn't tie up Allison's line in case the police needed to reach her. When the call came, Allison jumped to answer it. "Maybe that's some news." The others gathered around the phone and Allison whispered that it was Steve. As the conversation went on she kept nodding her head. Her nods were interrupted by "Oh?" and "Omigosh," and "Well, I declare." Fred, Connie and Dave sat motionless as they tried to figure out what was going on.

Allison replaced the phone, gave a huge sigh, and smiled at her cohorts. "Rufus Crandall has disappeared."

TWENTY-FOUR

DAVE LET OUT the Demon's victory yell—a cross between a gorilla's mating cry and a deranged smoke alarm. "We were right! Crandall is the culprit!"

Fred was more reserved. "Exactly what did Steve say?"

"Crandall didn't show up at the mill today," Allison said. "The secretary said this wasn't unusual. He came and went as he chose and never bothered to tell anybody unless he was going out of town on business. In fact she said he left early Thursday afternoon and didn't return. Then Mrs. Crandall admitted he didn't come home last night, but again, that wasn't unusual. She didn't elaborate, but Steve understood her to mean that he sometimes spent the night with a friend and went on to work from there.

"On Steve's urging, Mrs. Crandall went through her husband's closet and drawers. Steve said they had separate bedrooms and Mrs. Crandall said she seldom went into his room since the maid did the cleaning."

Allison paused to take a deep breath and to try to recollect exactly what Steve had said.

Dave was impatient. "And …?"

"And she thought some of his clothes were missing

but couldn't be sure since he kept some clothes at his friend's house."

"Did she name this friend?" Fred asked.

"No. Steve said she claimed she didn't know the name or location. Just that the relationship had been going on for several years."

Connie shook her head in disgust. "Men!" she muttered, and then laughed. "No aspersions on present company, of course."

Allison went on. "Steve asked about their financial situation and she said she really didn't know, but she thought they were well off. Rufus was very generous with money. He often bought her things, and he took her to Mexico several times during the past few months and told her to buy anything she wanted."

Fred was making notes as Allison talked and at this point he injected a comment. "Let me guess. He gave her cash to shop with—good old U.S. hundred dollar bills. They love American money in Mexico."

Connie nodded. "Sure. And she could easily get them changed into pesos. Who would suspect a sweet woman tourist of passing counterfeit bills?"

Allison agreed they were right. "Now do you want to hear the clincher?" The trio gave her their full attention. "Mrs. Crandall knew where her husband kept his passport. And it was gone!"

Dave whistled. "So our man is skipping the country. What is Steve going to do now?"

"He didn't say. I guess whatever police are supposed to do next."

Fred supplied the answer. "Alert the airlines, points of departure, border crossings. Broadcast his picture, description, car—the standard procedures. They'll find him."

Connie walked over behind her mother and gave her a worried squeeze. "But what if he hasn't left, and what if he finds out that Wally didn't kill Mom, and what if he thinks she knows about him? He may come after her."

Dave shook his head at his sister. "You worry too much. That man is long gone from here and Mom is perfectly safe."

Dave picked up the telephone book again. "Let's get on with the Ms. We've got to find the missing piece of the puzzle."

They worked their way through McClennan Auto Service, McRae Uphostery, Melvin's Pawn Shop and Merton Funeral Home, none of which had a significant F in their employ. Allison had stopped paying attention to their efforts, and Fred was on the phone to his own police station to be sure nothing drastic had happened in his absence. Connie read out the next business: Middleton Insurance. She made the call and went through her usual pitch. She scribbled as the names were given her. "Thank you. I appreciate your cooperation." She read the information to Dave. "Charles Middleton is the agency owner, but the on-site manager and top agent is Buford Franklin." Dave gave a disinterested nod. Connie tossed a wadded up piece of note paper at her brother. "Don't you get it? Franklin as in F!"

Dave came alive. He jumped up, grabbed Connie and whirled her around the room. Having missed their conversation, Allison stared at them with that mother look which poses the question, "Now what?"

Fred asked, "And what are we celebrating?"

"F-M," Dave crowed, "is Franklin-Middleton. Buford Franklin to be more specific."

"Oh, no. No." Allison flailed her hands wildly in protest. "You're wrong. It can't be Buck Franklin. Why he's the treasurer of the Art Council. I've known him forever. He's a friend of mine. He's the one who inadvertently took in the counterfeit bill. He's…." Allison left the word hanging somewhere in the middle of the room and buried her face in her hands.

Connie ran to her mother and patted her on the shoulder. "I know it hurts, Mom, to have your friends involved, but …."

"There's no 'but' about it. Buck is not a counterfeiter, and he certainly wouldn't shoot anybody. Why, Buck has been a lobbyist for gun control laws for years. After all," Allison finished lamely, "guns are bad for the insurance business."

"Mom," Dave said, "we're not accusing him of murder. Wally did the first killings and then Crandall probably killed Wally. But Franklin could have been involved in the money angle." Allison defiantly shook her head, but Dave persisted. "At least we could alert Steve and have him ask Franklin some questions."

Before the argument could go further, the phone rang

again. Allison seized it on the first ring. Anything was better than having an old friend accused of being a criminal. Buck may not have the greatest personality in the world, but Allison would bet her house on his honesty.

The voice on the other end of the line was distraught, but Allison welcomed it as a diversion from the world of crime. Here was a problem she could handle.

"Allison, you have to help me," Susan Webb pleaded. "Mr. Forster insists I get the interim grade report in before I leave this afternoon and I haven't the foggiest notion how to do it."

"All right, now don't panic," Allison spoke soothingly to her substitute teacher. "I'd forgotten about the school board meeting Monday, and he likes to give them the latest grades. Tell him I'll come in early Monday morning and do it."

"I can't. That is, he's gone—said he had another meeting. I thought I could ask another teacher to help me, but one of the students stayed after class to discuss a paper she's doing and by the time we finished, everyone else was gone."

Allison took a deep breath. She knew Susan was a good teacher, but the substitute didn't work enough to keep up with the grading system. "It's very simple. I'll walk you through it. You just have to average the numbers in my grade book. You'll notice that the test scores are on a separate sheet and …."

"But Allison," Susan interrupted. "I'm supposed to

meet my husband in a few minutes. We're going to his mother's for the weekend. He'll be upset if I'm late. Couldn't you come in and do it? I hate to ask. But Mr. Forster was really insistent that the report be on his desk tonight." Susan's voice dropped to a whimper. "And I just don't have the time."

"Don't worry about it," Allison said. "I'll come in." She wanted to add that she was tired of the principal's ultimatums, of a medieval grading system, and especially of whiny substitutes. Instead she said, "You go ahead. Have a nice weekend."

Three heads turned her way when she hung up the phone. Fred was the first to speak. "And just where is it you're planning to go?"

"To the school. I have to do some silly report. It won't take me fifteen minutes. And I'll come right straight home."

Fred shook his head and worry lines creased his forehead. "You can't go anywhere in your condition."

"My condition is just fine." Allison tapped the side of her head. "This little scratch is nothing to worry about. I'll be back in a jiffy." She laughed and added, "I promise."

Allison snatched her parka and purse and headed for the door before remembering her car lay scattered in a thousand pieces next to a charred cabin. She tiptoed shyly back into the den. "Ah, Connie, may I borrow your car?"

"No," Connie replied, "you may not. You've been a little hard on cars lately." The young girl grinned at her mother. "But if you insist on going, I'll drive you."

Fred jumped up. "How about letting me drive you? I'd love to see your school anyway."

Allison waved him back. "You've seen one school, you've seen them all. You stay here and make yourself useful. See what you can find for dinner. You like to brag about your cooking skills. It's time you showed us some proof."

Fred gave in. "All right. If you have anything decent in your freezer, I'll fix a meal that will make your toes tingle."

As Susan had said, the school was deserted. There were no cars in the parking lot, no lights peeking into the dusk, and the empty yellow buses were lined up in formation. The only key Allison had to the school was to the back gym door, so she directed Connie to drive around that way. She unlocked the door and switched on a light as they stepped inside. Allison loved the gym. She had a good feeling every time she opened the door, caught sight of the hoops, the benches, the "Demon" banner. Today was no exception. This was her peaceful little corner of the world.

She breathed deeply of the gym's aromas. Even though it was empty, Allison could still smell the funky athletic shoes, the adolescent bodies steeped with sweat and hormones, the unique odor of much-used basketballs and volleyballs. It reminded her of how much she loved her job. Here she felt warm and youthful—and needed. She related well to her young charges and although they made jokes about her being the oldest gym teacher in the state, she knew they liked and respected her.

Last year Mr. Forster had suggested she relinquish her gym activities to a younger teacher. In return he offered her the position of student counselor. She'd actually considered it for a few minutes, but decided she couldn't trade the gym floor for a stuffy office. She knew she'd made the right decision, at least for now.

The gym was connected to the classrooms by a half-flight of stairs and a hallway. Connie went on ahead of her, clicked on the hall light, and waited for her mother. "Quiet as a tomb," she said. "If you're sure you'll be all right, I think I'll scoot out to the drugstore. I packed in a hurry and forgot some things."

"Sure. Go ahead. Lock the gym door as you go out. When I finish, I'll come down and wait on you."

"Good. Be back soon."

Allison hurried to her classroom and wasted no time tackling the interim grade report. It was a "Forster" original—a form he had created and foisted on his long-suffering teaching staff. It took longer to complete than she had anticipated. She glanced at her watch, and reached for her purse. In her hurry, she brushed against some papers Susan had left on the desk. She gathered them up and started to slip them into the top drawer. I'll see what they are Monday, she thought. Right now I'm going to leave this report in the office and get out of here.

But as she opened the drawer, she saw a pile of dollar bills and a note—*Raffle money. $16.00 S. Webb.* "Oh, no," she mumbled in exasperation. "Susan should know we can't leave money in our desks. Now I'll have to take that to the office too." Allison knew the money was from raffle tickets the students were selling, but she'd forgotten what they were raising money for this time. It didn't matter. Mr. Forster was adamant that all money had to be placed in a bank deposit bag and taken to his office. She knew his office would be locked, but maybe she could slide it under his door. She scooped up the money and the report, turned out her light and headed toward the principal's office.

The outer office door was never locked. Here, the secretary reigned. The area also housed extra supplies as well as straight chairs for unfortunate students who waited their appointment with the executioner. Allison flicked on the light and searched the shelves in vain for the slim plastic bank bag she needed. She was considering taking the money home for safekeeping when she noticed that the door to the inner office was slightly ajar.

Allison had no intention of snooping when she opened the door. She was simply looking for a bank bag. She could leave the money and the report on Mr. Forster's desk and then lock the door on her way out.

The light from the outer office made a path to the desk and illuminated its surface. To her delight a bank deposit bag lay there. She laid down the report and picked up the bag. She was surprised to find it quite heavy. Wow, she thought, somebody is really selling raffle tickets. She zipped the bag open to squeeze in her few dollars and Susan's note. As she pushed the stack of bills back to make room, she noticed that the pictures didn't match. Instead of President Washington's visage, Allison stared into the face of Ben Franklin. It was the same face on the same kind of bill that had given her trouble at the grocery store!

A shock went through Allison as real as if she had touched an electric fence. She dropped the bank bag, stuffed Susan's money into her pocket, and backed away from the desk. At first, her mind refused to believe what her eyes had seen. She had to be sure.

She held her breath, stepped back to the desk, picked up the black bag, and forced herself to examine its contents. She rubbed one of the bills between her fingers and compared it with one in her pocket. She flipped through them and determined they were all hundreds. Her brain reeled with the thought of holding thousands of dollars in her hands. What is it doing here? She took two deep breaths, tried to calm down. It didn't make sense. Thousands of dollars in my school? In Mr. Forster's office? It took several seconds but she had to finally accept what she knew was the truth. She was holding thousands of dollars in counterfeit bills.

Again something like an electric current raced through her mind. This time the shock unveiled the last piece of the puzzle. She quickly re-zipped the bag and laid it back in exactly the same spot where she'd found it.

I knew the kids were wrong about Buck Franklin, she thought. F-M isn't Franklin-Middleton, but Forster-Madison.

How could they have missed it? She remembered hearing Dave instruct Connie to read out the names of all the businesses and companies which started with M. He hadn't said anything about schools.

Allison started behind the desk to reach for the phone. She had to call 9-1-1 and get the police out here. She had to hand the money over to them and then they needed to find Mr. Forster. Before she got around to the phone, a shadow blocked the light from the outer office. She glanced up.

Mr. Forster smiled.

TWENTY-FIVE

BACK AT THE ALDRIDGE HOUSE Fred was busy preparing dinner when the phone rang. Dave grabbed it up in mid-ring. Fred slammed the oven door on his rump roast and vegetables, perched on the arm of the couch, and stared question marks at the boy. Dave mouthed "Steve" to him. It was maddening for Fred to stand by and watch Dave as he listened and nodded, listened and smiled, listened and shot his eyebrows up. Fred wanted to assert his authority and snatch the instrument away, but he had to remind himself that he had no authority here. He was simply a friend of the family. Fred held his tongue but promised himself when this mess was over, he would change that. He planned to become more than a friend.

Steve must have paused for a breath because Dave turned and gave him a quick summary. "They're on Crandall's trail. Houston."

Fred scowled. He wanted details.

Dave listened again and then he told Steve of their latest theory. "The other person you want is Buck Franklin of Middleton Insurance. If Crandall didn't kill Wally than Franklin did."

When Dave hung up the phone, Fred pounced on his last words. "Steve doesn't think Crandall killed Wally?"

Dave shook his head. "Couldn't have. Crandall was identified as a passenger on a flight to Houston that left Raleigh at five yesterday afternoon. At five o'clock Wally was still alive and had just left Mom and Gil to be fried in a burning cabin."

Fred chewed on the new information and then asked, "What else did Steve say?"

"They think he's still in Houston. At least he's not taken any flights out. He may be waiting until the heat's off to skip across the border."

"Is that what Steve said?" Fred demanded. "Crandall is waiting until the *heat's off?*"

Dave shrugged. "Not exactly. Those were my words."

"That's what I thought. Now, once again, what did Steve say?"

Properly chastised, Dave sat up straight and tried to repeat Steve's message word-for-word. "He said he was probably still in Houston. The police there are going to splash…." Dave paused. "I'm pretty sure he said 'splash' his picture all over the news and someone may spot him."

"And what did he say when you told him about Franklin?"

"He said they would question him." Dave squirmed and scratched his head. "You know, Mom's going to be mad. She's convinced Buck is innocent. I may be in the doghouse."

"You did right," Fred said. "You had to tell your suspicions. I'll smooth it over with your mother." Fred looked at the clock on the fireplace mantle and checked it against his watch. "And where in the world are those two. They should be back by now. We shouldn't have let her go. She might still be weak from yesterday's ordeal."

Dave walked over to the window and stared at the fleeting daylight. "But Connie's with her. I'm sure they'll be home soon."

The phone rang again. This time Fred was closer and he jerked it up. His face paled as he repeated the words he'd just heard. "She's alone at the school?" He listened a few more seconds, growled, "I'll be right there," and slammed the phone down.

"What?" Dave questioned.

"Connie left your mother to run to Perry's drugstore, and now she's got a flat tire. Come on. We'll pick her up and then go to the school."

Dave hesitated. "I better wait here in case there's more news. The drug store is easy to find. You just go east from here down to Main Street. Turn left, and it'll be on your left."

FRED PICKED UP CONNIE, and she directed him to the school by back streets. It was a quicker way to the gym entrance.

"That's strange," she said as they pulled up. "Mom said she'd wait for me here when she finished, but I don't see her." Fred stopped the car. They jumped out and Connie tried the door. "She insisted I lock it when I went out, but she kept the key. Wonder where she can be?"

"Maybe she's still working. Where's her room?"

Connie pointed to a row of windows past the gym just above their heads. "It's one of those windows. I'm not sure which one, and I don't see any lights. It's actually a first floor room, but here behind the school the ground slopes down and makes the windows above eye level."

"And so we can't see if she's in there or not. Well, we can't just stand around and wait for her to come out."

"What else can we do? Want me to try some yodeling?"

"I've got a better idea." Fred headed back to the car. "I'll drive up and down close to the building so I'll be right below the windows. If I drive slowly and toot my horn, maybe we'll get her attention. You keep looking at the windows to see if she peeps out. If she does, wave to let her know we're waiting for her."

"All right," Connie agreed. "It's worth a try."

MR. FORSTER CONTINUED SMILING as he entered his office. "Well, hello, Mrs. Aldridge. This is a surprise. I understood you were home sick today."

Allison returned his smile, determined not to panic. After all, he didn't know that she knew. "I was. But Mrs. Webb called and needed some assistance. I came to your office to leave the grade report and some raffle money." Allison edged out from behind the desk and took a step toward the principal. She waited for him to move out of the doorway so she could leave. He didn't. Allison stalled. "Susan, that is, Mrs. Webb, said you'd gone to a meeting."

He nodded. "But I left in a hurry and forgot the school's bank deposit. I came back for it." He reached over and picked up the black bag. He eyed her carefully. "Did you include your money in here?"

"Oh, no," Allison answered too quickly. "I still have it." She dug the wadded bills from her pocket and thrust them in his direction. He made no move to take the money, and Allison let her hand drop.

Mr. Forster waved the bank bag at Allison. "Why didn't you put it in?"

Allison caught her breath, but managed to say, "I decided to bring it back on Monday."

"Why?"

He's playing with me, Allison thought. He knows I saw the money. I've got to get out of here. But how? It was a small office; the desk sat in the center of the room, a potted rubber plant beside it, a row of windows to her back, and Mr. Forster between her and the door. Allison knew she had to say something, anything, to keep his attention while she planned her escape. "The bank bag seemed rather full."

Mr. Forster's lips spread in what Allison could only describe as a sneer. He took several steps around the desk and then came toward her. "And you know what's in the bag." It wasn't a question.

"How would I know?" As she sparred with her tormentor, questions played tag in her head. Could she vault the potted plant and distract him enough to get out the door? How desperate was Mr. Forster to keep his secret? Desperate enough to kill her? How long before Connie became concerned and alerted someone?

Allison watched in horror as Mr. Forster made a quick half-turn, slammed the door shut, and snapped the lock. The office was plunged into dark shadows. Outside, the late afternoon sun was flirting with the tops of long-leaf pines, allowing only flickers of light to sneak into the room. There was enough light, however, for Allison to see Mr. Forster drop the bank bag and seize an old-fashioned school bell that had anchored the corner of his desk for years. It had a long metal handle but no clapper. It was heavy. It was solid. It was potentially deadly. He swung the bell threateningly and answered her previous question. "You know what's in the bag because you're a snoop. That's why I told Wally to get rid of you. You were getting too close."

Allison gasped. "You told Wally to kill me?"

"The fool. I hate people who don't do as they're told. Life is so much simpler when people follow orders."

For a moment Allison had the absurd thought that she should defend Wally. He certainly had done his best to carry out the order. She knew firsthand of Mr.

Forster's intolerance for sloppy work. She also knew his obsession with tidiness. He abhorred an unfinished task. There was no question in her mind that he intended to finish what Wally hadn't. Her eyes played leapfrog from the bell, to the door, to her place trapped behind his desk. She contemplated scurrying under the desk, but that would only tighten the trap since it had no through opening. Apparently the principal disliked visitors seeing his skinny legs under the desk.

As he stepped closer, Allison thought she heard a car horn. Had she imagined it? No. There it was again. Not loud. Just a tap, tap, tap. And it was getting closer. Allison studied Mr. Forster's face. He gave no indication that he had heard it. Allison continued her retreat, backing into the rubber plant, putting as much room as possible between the two of them. The horn honked again. It must be Connie trying to get my attention, she thought. I've got to let her know I'm in here. And I've got to stay alive until help arrives. She had no idea how that help would appear. Would Connie realize she was in danger and call Fred? Maybe she had already called him. Maybe he would burst through the door like Superman and whisk her away.

Mr. Forster continued toward her. Allison backed away. What could she use to defend herself?

As Mr. Forster took another step closer, Allison gripped the back of his desk chair and maneuvered it in front of her. She started wheeling it slowly back and forth keeping it between herself and her stalker. Mr. Forster smiled scornfully at her pitiful defense. She tried talking again. "You can't get away with killing me. The police know where I am. If I disappear, they'll come after you." Allison felt sure her kids would eventually figure out the identity of F-M.

"Oh, you're not going to disappear, Mrs. Aldridge. You're going to stay right here at the school. Someone will find your body at the bottom of the gym stairs where you fell and hit your head." Mr. Forster gave a strained laugh. "You really should take better care of yourself. Yesterday's injury was worse than you realized. It could make you very, very dizzy." He took a step closer. She wiggled the chair. "And if the police care to question me, I'll be at home—where I went immediately following my meeting. But enough chit-chat. It's getting close to my dinnertime, and I'm hungry."

Mr. Forster lifted his right foot and gave the chair a hefty kick. It slammed into Allison's abdomen, knocked her feet out from under her and landed her against the rubber plant. She clutched at the corner of the desk in a desperate attempt to right herself. At the same time she heard the toot of a horn again. She glanced at the windows behind her. She had to get the attention of whoever was out there.

The principal grabbed the back of his desk chair and sent it spinning to the other side of the room.

Allison's fingers touched and then grasped a piece of petrified wood which the principal used as a paper weight. She raised the wooden rock as her adversary leaned over her.

TWENTY-SIX

DAVE HATED WAITING, and he especially hated waiting when he didn't know what he was waiting for. Steve had given him all the information they had. It might be hours before the police finished questioning Franklin. What was he supposed to do in the meantime? He decided now was the time to take his college roommate's advice, "When in doubt, eat." He started for the cookie jar, forgetting he had emptied it during lunch. Oh well, he thought, saltines and peanut butter will do just as well. He downed a half-dozen crackers and a Dr. Pepper and was wondering what kind of ice cream might be in the freezer when the phone rang.

This time it was Martha. Her words tumbled out like gushing water. "Big news! Steve asked me to call. He went out to pick up the big fish, but he's not home. They're setting up a drag net. We're running to the finish line, Dave. It's almost over. Is your mother there? I want to tell her the news."

She paused just long enough to hear Dave's, "No."

"That's okay. You can tell her. Crandall was picked up at a motel in Houston—with a suitcase crammed full of funny money. And he started squealing the minute they handcuffed him—hoping to get off easy. He…"

Dave interrupted her with a big, "Whoa, let's back up a little. So Crandall confirmed Franklin as Wally's killer?"

"No, no, no!" Martha nearly screamed into the phone. "You were all wrong about Franklin. Crandall's partner is Alvin Forster—he's the brains behind the whole outfit. He got Wally and Leroy to make the money, he ordered Wally to kill the others, and then he killed Wally. The only reason Crandall is still alive is because he flew the coop before the axe fell."

Dave was trying to make sense of all the information Martha was throwing at him. "Alvin Forster? Who's he?" Then it hit him. "Forster? You mean Mr. Forster, the principal at Madison?"

"Yeah. Can you believe that? Quite a role model for his students! Can you imagine the fallout from this? Those students will…."

Dave didn't care about the students right now. He wanted to know where Forster was right now. "Omigosh!" he whispered into the phone. "What if he's at the school? Mom's there."

Martha exhaled slowly. "What did you say?"

"My mother is at the school. Connie took her and then had a flat tire. Fred went to pick them both up. But none of them are home yet. They may all be in danger!"

"Oh, my God," Martha moaned. "We're on our way." The phone clicked, and Dave dropped his face in his hands.

His paralysis lasted only a moment. Dave was a

young man of action. No way was he going to sit around when his family needed him. He picked up the phone again and dialed. Holliston had only one taxi company, and it was not noted for speedy responses, but Dave figured he might luck out. It's too early for the Friday night drinkers, he thought, and most of the town's offices had closed for the day. The dispatcher sounded reassuring. "Be maybe five, maybe ten minutes."

It was seven minutes—the longest seven minutes Dave ever remembered. He waited on the sidewalk and spent the time going over and over the unbelievable thought that his old principal had become both a counterfeiter and a killer. And he closed his eyes at the terrifying thought of the danger his mother might be in. It had been a long time since he'd prayed for anything, but the words came without hesitation. "Please God, take care of my mom."

FRED DROVE SLOWLY, tapping his horn. Connie walked alongside the car and stared at the windows a floor above them. She saw nothing—no lights—no shadows. She motioned to Fred to stop; he lowered the window and she stuck her head in. "A little louder. Make like a lovelorn moose." Fred complied and out came a long, mournful cry for attention. Connie jumped back and pointed her finger. "Up there. I saw a movement. Look!"

Fred scrambled out of the car and looked where

Connie was pointing. "I don't see anything. It's dark, just like all the other rooms."

"I know I saw something. She's in there. Why doesn't she look out the window?"

Allison was well aware of the horn but could not acknowledge it right then. She was too busy avoiding contact with what police would call, "a blunt instrument." Her attacker was leaning over the desk within striking distance. Allison threw back her right arm, pivoted around toward the windows and pitched the petrified wood-turned-rock with all the strength she had left. The rock found its mark, smashed the office window, and landed on top of the horn-blowing car.

Mr. Forster laughed. He again raised his weapon.

FRED SNATCHED UP the rock, and vaulted onto the hood of the car. He was now on eye-level with the smashed window. He stretched his short frame enough to see through the cracked glass. What he saw were two phantom forms: one crouching, the other towering above.

Fred dropped his head out of sight, broke out some more glass with the rock, and shouted, "Drop your weapon and step back or I'll shoot!"

THE VOICE IMMOBILIZED the bell and the arm holding it. Allison held her breath. She stared at the black shape hovering over her. The voice came again. "Move back and put your hands up. Now!"

Mr. Forster did exactly that. He stepped away from Allison, dropped his weapon on the floor, raised his hands, and waited. Fred peered through the window at the shadow leaning against the desk. "Allison," Fred shouted, "are you all right?"

"Yes. Oh, yes. I am now," Allison sobbed. Anything else she may have said was drowned out by the sound of sirens.

Dave arrived at the school just in time to see the principal of Madison Middle School being led away in handcuffs. Then he saw Fred deep in conversation with Steve. Finally he spied his mother and sister huddling together beside a patrol car. Dave sprinted to join them, enclosed them both in the same embrace, and gave his mother a resounding kiss on her cheek. "Martha was right, Mom," he said. "It'll take a larger police force than Holliston has to keep you out of trouble."

STEVE ASSIGNED two officers to secure the premises while the other cars formed a cavalcade back to the police station. Connie and Dave rode with one of the officers. Fred and Allison brought up the rear. Steve had briefly explained to Fred the accusations made against Forster, but Fred still didn't understand how Allison managed to get in the middle of things again. He felt like shaking her for being so careless or so foolhardy. He wanted her to tell him every detail of what happened. Then he would make her swear nothing like that would ever happen again. But most of all he wanted to hold her tight, to tell her everything was all right, and to say that he never wanted to come that close to losing her again. He'd say all that later, and a lot more. Right now they had to make their statements and get home to his roast.

ALLISON JUST WANTED to crawl into bed, cover up her head, and blot out the last hour. But the delectable aroma of roast beef with onions changed her mind. Her appetite returned, and with it, her curiosity. They had given their statements individually at the police station, and now she wanted to hear exactly what the others had said. They, in turn, needed to know how she had become entangled in her latest dance with death.

The conversation and the food ran out about the same time. Dave stabbed the last sliver of beef and beamed at Fred. "First you cook a fabulous meal, and then you save my mother. You're quite a guy. Good thing you had your gun with you."

Fred propped his hands under his chin and winked at Allison. "Oh, but I didn't," he said. "I seldom carry a gun when I'm off duty. My only weapon was the rock which had just put a dent in the hood of my car. Luckily, it was too dark for Forster to tell the difference."

SATURDAY MORNING found the Aldridge family and friend sitting around in a haze of inactivity. They were talked out and worn out, brain dead and dead on their feet. The coffeepot was their only link to life. Dave and

Connie were making noises about returning to school—
something about needing to study for exams. Allison
wondered aloud if she could ever return to Madison
Middle School again, and Fred said he was thinking of
taking her home with him. Any romance connected to
that statement was dissipated when he added, "I have
a cozy cell which might keep you out of trouble."

Then Steve called and asked if they would like to
hear an abridged version of Rufus Crandall's statement.
They scurried to get dressed. Dave made a quick run to
Krispy Kreme and Connie put on another pot of coffee.
They were ready and waiting when Steve arrived.
Between sips and chews, he told them the story accord-
ing to Crandall.

"Not unexpectedly, Crandall laid everything at
Forster's feet. The counterfeiting began when Wally
Stitson tried to match his artistic talents against Uncle
Sam's. Wally succeeded in passing a phony twenty at
a local service station, but then Forster, who was right
behind Wally at the cash register, was given the twenty
in change when he paid with a fifty. When Forster
examined the bill, an idea took shape.

"He remembered Wally from school. Instead of
turning him over to the police, Forster contacted him
and struck up a deal. In return for his silence, Wally was
to supply Forster with counterfeit money. Forster suggested ways Wally could improve the quality of the
bills and told him to find some way to make them look
old. Since Wally worked in the office at the Valley Mill,

he had access to computers and copying machines. He had also struck up an acquaintance with Leroy. Leroy knew about chemicals and dyes and, most important, he worked alone. No one dared to enter his maintenance shop. So Wally recruited Leroy, and together they set up an assembly line for funny money."

"I'm not trying to excuse Leroy," Allison said, "but, in a way, I can understand why he would agree to it. He was worried about the plant moving to Mexico. He would lose his job and because of Malvina's illness, they had little savings."

"I can see that," Dave said. "But how did Crandall get involved?"

Steve went on. "Crandall said he became suspicious about some of Wally's movements and soon discovered what was going on behind his back. He decided he also wanted a piece of the action. The four of them worked out a deal. Wally and Leroy would take orders for their bills from the other two. In exchange, they would be paid ten percent of the value in real money. They agreed that no money should be passed in or around Holliston, so as to avoid local scrutiny. Crandall couldn't explain how one of the bills ended up at the art show. The plan was for Crandall and Forster to pass the bills in their travels. Most of Crandall's went to Mexico while Forster took some really nice vacations. Both of them were accumulating a pile destined for Europe later on.

"Unknown to any of the others, Leroy was noting the transactions on his calendar. When Leroy found out that

Malvina had given the calendar to Allison, he panicked and told Wally and Crandall about it. That's when Wally searched Allison's classroom and came up empty-handed. The next day Crandall, not trusting Leroy to take care of the situation, ordered Wally to break into Allison's house. However, Malvina saw him and threatened to call the police. Her unplanned kidnapping left Wally in a quandary. He told Crandall about it, but he didn't dare let Leroy know what had happened. Nevertheless Leroy did suspect Wally in Malvina's disappearance and confronted him behind the mill. That was the argument Professor Keyes witnessed on Saturday."

Steve got up, stretched, poured himself another cup of coffee. Four pairs of eyes followed his every movement, but no one said anything. They waited patiently until Steve settled himself back on the sofa, and the saga continued.

"At this point Crandall told Forster about the missing calendar and about Malvina. He insists that it was Forster who ordered Wally to dispose of both Malvina and Leroy, and to do whatever was necessary to get the calendar back. So Wally broke in here to search for the calendar, but was interrupted when Allison came home early. Crandall wasn't sure what happened between Wally and Leroy on Sunday, but assumed that Wally carried out Forster's orders and made it look like an accident. Wally did tell him that when he returned to the cabin Sunday afternoon, Malvina was already dead and he buried her. By the way, the medical examiner confirmed that Malvina died of a heart attack.

"Crandall said he thought killing Professor Keyes was a desperate act on Wally's part to prevent his being identified. Crandall knew the end was coming, went home, grabbed his stash of money and his passport, and drove to the nearest airport. That's the end of his story. We have to piece the rest together."

"That shouldn't be hard to do," Fred said. "Forster admitted to ordering Wally to kill Allison. We can assume then that Wally came here, saw her leave, saw Gil behind her, and followed them both to the cabin. Wally probably thought he had succeeded in his assignment to kill Allison. Forster found out differently when his secretary told him Allison had called in and was taking another day off. He may have called Wally to meet him in the park, maybe said he'd help with an escape plan. Whatever was said, we know that Forster killed Wally, and then tried to hide his body and his car."

"And my encounter with Forster yesterday," Allison said, "was one of those weird quirks of timing. He had no idea I'd be at the school. And until I saw the bag of money, I wasn't the least suspicious of him."

As the story came to an end, Connie seemed to voice everyone's thoughts. "Thank God, it's over. But Holliston will never be the same."

ON SUNDAY AFTERNOON things crawled back to near normalcy. After making their mother promise again and again to stay out of trouble, Connie and Dave packed up and headed back to school. Allison found last week's newspaper and started reading the used car and cell phone ads.

Fred took a trip to the grocery store to restock Allison's dwindling food supplies. When he came back, he fixed tuna salad sandwiches and stirred up a box of brownie mix. The tantalizing aroma from the oven lured Allison to the kitchen. She crossed the room and gave him a hug. "Are you trying to impress me with your culinary talents?"

"What I would really like to impress you with is another talent of mine."

"And that would be?"

He lifted her face to his. The ensuing kiss answered her question.

WHEN FRED FINALLY LEFT for home, Allison collapsed in the recliner. The painting, *Breakthrough,* she'd bought at the art show seemed to smile at her. "Yes, indeed," she said to the picture. "I'd say we had a breakthrough."

She reached for her day-planner on the coffee table, and studied the rest of February. She took a red pencil and circled two dates. The twenty-eighth was the annual Spring Flower Show. It seemed early, but that was the purpose of the show—to tantalize people with all the possibilities of the season. Maybe she could find some unusual flowers to plant on Professor Keyes's grave.

Her eyes backed up to the fourteenth. She circled it twice. She hoped it was going to be a special day.

SURE ENOUGH, IT WAS. Fred showed up at her doorstep with his hands full. "I couldn't decide between the deluxe box of Valentine chocolates and the Passion-Red roses. So I brought both. And," he added as her eyes lit up, "a little something else." He shifted the roses and patted his jacket pocket where Allison caught a glimpse of a small jeweler's box. She snatched him into the house and quickly shut the door.